I0576605

Sarge and Pickett carefully got the blinds open without stirring up too much dust, then managed to get both windows pushed up about halfway before the windows stuck.

At least the room was now bathed in light, showing off the swirling dust they did stir up. And there was a slight breeze going through the room and down the hall toward the open front door.

Then when Sarge turned around to look at the room, he almost choked.

And beside him, Pickett gasped.

One full wall was covered in Polaroid pictures of a blonde girl. A large bed faced the picture wall.

There were hundreds of pictures on that wall, all clearly old, many yellowing as old Polaroid pictures tended to do. Most of the pictures were nude shots of a smiling, laughing young blonde.

"And just when I thought this house couldn't get any creepier," Sarge said.

ALSO BY DEAN WESLEY SMITH

ALSO BY DEAN WESLEY SMITH

Cold Poker Gang Mysteries

Kill Game

Cold Call

Calling Dead

Dead Hand

Freedom

High

Bank Call

Heaven's Up

Blind Game

Bottom Feeders

Doc Hill Thrillers

Dead Money

The Road Back

BURN CARD

A Cold Poker Gang Mystery

DEAN WESLEY SMITH

Burn Card

Copyright © 2021 by Dean Wesley Smith

All rights reserved

First published in a different form in *Smith's Monthly* #44, May 2017
Published by WMG Publishing
Cover and layout copyright © 2021 by WMG Publishing
Cover art copyright © by gorgev/Depositphotos
ISBN-13: 978-1-56146-036-6
ISBN-10: 1-56146-036-2

This book is licensed for your personal enjoyment only. All rights reserved. This is a work of fiction. All characters and events portrayed in this book are fictional, and any resemblance to real people or incidents is purely coincidental. This book, or parts thereof, may not be reproduced in any form without permission.

AUTHOR'S NOTE

The characters in this book are fictional and any similarity to any person, alive or dead, is purely accidental. This is a work of fiction.

BURN CARD

Burn Card:

The top card on the deck after the original cards are dealt to each player in a game of Hold'em poker. That top card is mucked (or burned) each time before laying out the flop, turn, and river cards, so in case it was seen, no one player has an advantage. In other words, a card is burned each time to ensure the integrity of the game.

PART ONE

The House of Mystery

PROLOGUE

June 12th, 1977
Las Vegas, Nevada

Cathy Wendt smiled at her kid brother, Kevin, as he did his best to stand on his head against the wall in the hallway. Mom hated it when he did that because it left scuff marks on the paint, so this time he had taken off his shoes. Didn't much matter, the scuff marks were already all the way along the light blue paint. And every time Mom saw them, she got angry.

The hallway had a light blue shag carpet on the floor that helped Kevin with the padding on the top of his head a little.

Cathy thought it cute that a five-year-old wanted to be a gymnast when he grew up. But she had a hunch her little brother was going to be able to do anything he wanted as he got older.

He was that smart and that driven. And that was clear already at five.

She moved from her bedroom door to help hold his legs

steady. She was five-five and Kevin, standing on his head, already came up to her chest. Wow was he growing.

"Now point your toes and straighten your legs and you'll have it."

Kevin did and she let go.

Sure enough, he held himself there for a good three seconds before tumbling to the carpet. He was smiling like he had just gotten the best birthday present ever.

"You keep practicing," Cathy said as she headed down the carpeted stairs.

Her mom was working on something that smelled heavenly for dinner already, even though it was only one in the afternoon. A pot roast or something that needed all afternoon to cook, more than likely.

Her mom was such a good cook, it was amazing to Cathy that she and her mother both kept as thin as they did. Luckily, Cathy took after her mother, not only with the long golden-blonde hair, but the thin, short body.

But Mom had her other issues. Cathy didn't want to think about them.

And clearly Dad didn't help. His job kept him away often at nights. Cathy hated how he came home smelling at times.

And what he made her do.

She put that out of her mind. It no longer mattered.

Cathy was going to miss her little brother and her mom's cooking. Not much else.

And she was going to miss the good things about her mom. Not the bad things, not the ugly things, but the good things. She promised herself she would do that, remember only the good.

Ben would be worth it.

He was her love. Her soul mate, as they were starting to call it.

She went into the large, bright kitchen and kissed her mom on the cheek. "Smells fantastic. I'm headed over to pick up Ben and then we're going to the library to research colleges some more."

That was the cover story they had agreed on for today.

Her mom nodded. "Dinner at six sharp," she said without looking away from the potato she was peeling.

"I'll be here," Cathy said, making her voice sound bright and happy as she took the car keys off the hook near the back door and headed out.

"Bring Ben if he wants to come," her mother said.

Cathy said, "I'll ask him and tell him how good it smells."

Cathy didn't make it to dinner.

Not that one, not any dinner with her family going forward.

Cathy Wendt vanished into thin air.

CHAPTER ONE

June 10th, 2017
Las Vegas, Nevada

Sometimes solving cold cases was actually easy. Only sometimes, but clearly they had drawn one of those easy ones this time.

Retired Detective Debra Pickett just stood beside her partner, best friend, and lover, Retired Detective Sarge Carson.

They both said nothing. Just stared at the scene in front of them.

They were in a basement of a home near the University. The home had been built in the 1960s and had an unfinished basement with a furnace in it and not much else.

The floor was hard dirt covered in gravel and in one side of the large, extremely dry room was a wooden rocking chair that looked like it had been used a lot over the years from the wear patterns on the arms and headrest area.

A dried-up corpse of an older man sat in the rocking chair,

his gray hair down over his shirt and his teeth yellow. His eye sockets were empty and seemed to just be staring.

The guy had on brown slacks that had stained from his body drying, a dress shirt with the sleeves rolled up, and his feet were still in his slippers.

If Pickett had to guess, he had been dead for almost a year and had mummified in the dry air of the desert basement. Right now, even though it was well over a hundred outside, the air down here held a fairly steady temperature.

And no moisture at all. None.

Beside her, Sarge said nothing, just stared.

She had seen this kind of thing before. Never helped the sleep for the next few nights, that was for sure.

Sometimes a case just sort of solved itself. Hard to imagine that might happen with cold cases that had remained unsolved for decades. But it did happen. She couldn't believe this was one of those cases.

At the Cold Poker Gang meeting last week, she and Sarge and Robin had been given a very, very cold case of a girl by the name of Cathy Wendt who had vanished almost forty years ago exactly.

Neither she nor Sarge nor Robin, Pickett's old partner when she was on the force, had thought they had any hope of solving this one. Neither did any of the other retired detectives at the game that night.

But they took the case file just to go through the motions.

A forty-year-old cold case seldom got any traction. Just too much time had passed, too many possible witnesses had died, too much evidence had been lost.

After forty years, nothing much would be left.

They all three knew that.

Plus the records in the 1970s were all paper. And more than

likely most of the ones they would need would have been destroyed decades before.

Robin had just shaken her head and said to call her if they needed her help. Her computer work was not much use for forty-year-old cases.

But Pickett and Sarge had both decided to give the case a day or two of legwork before tossing the file on the bar at the Cold Poker Gang meeting room with the other unsolved files.

They did get one break and managed to talk to Cathy's kid brother, Kevin, a dealer down at a small casino off the Strip.

He had been five when Cathy vanished and all they learned from him was how it had destroyed his family. And how angry he was at his sister for vanishing and leaving them.

For leaving him with "those people," as he called his parents.

Deep down angry.

Then he told them about how, when he was sixteen, his mother killed herself in her kitchen. His father, who was never home much anyway, had stayed away even more after Cathy vanished and vanished completely when Kevin was twelve. He had no idea what ever happened to his father and didn't care.

Mostly they learned how much Kevin hated Cathy for leaving him.

And that was all he could give them.

So Pickett and Sarge decided to see if the boyfriend was still alive.

The police at the time had interviewed Cathy's boyfriend, Ben March.

Turned out he was the one who had called in that she hadn't shown up for an afternoon date with him. He had gotten worried, called her mom, they had both gotten even more worried, and within a day the police were in full search mode since she was only seventeen.

They never found a clue for days until the family car was discovered at the airport. Nothing suspicious and the police had no idea who had put the car there.

That was long before security cameras in those sorts of places.

The missing person's case of Cathy Wendt went cold quickly after that and had remained that way for forty years.

Not one clue, no one remembered it.

It had been ten in the morning on the second day of them looking into the case when they had gone to Ben March's home and knocked on the door. The day was already hot and clearly the old home was hot inside as well.

The house had clearly seen better days. The grass hadn't been mowed in a year at least and was nothing more than a few dried weeds and dirt now. There was a notice dated last winter on the door that the power had been shut off.

The drapes were pulled so as they walked around the house they could see nothing.

They knocked on a few neighbors' doors to ask if anyone had seen the man who owned that house. No one had in a very long time.

And Ben's only car was still in the driveway, one tire flat and a layer of dust coating it.

"You thinking what I'm thinking?" Pickett had asked Sarge as they stood near their car and stared at the rundown and abandoned home.

Sarge had nodded. "He's in there. More than likely dead for some time."

They headed back to their condo in the Ogden and had a friend on the force to actually look at Ben March's credit cards and bank accounts while they had checked his history.

Nothing had been touched for almost a year and he had no employment they could find.

Pickett thought that Ben had also been a victim to Cathy's vanishing as much as Cathy's family. He had dropped out of school the same time she vanished. There were no other records from the time that they could find on him. Looked like he had stayed at home with his parents until they died ten years later and he inherited the house.

It seemed, as far as any records they could find, that he had never left it.

"It's amazing how one tragedy can lead to so many others," Pickett said, shaking her head.

All Sarge could do was nod. Both of them had been detectives for long enough that they had seen this kind of thing more than they wanted to ever admit.

And they both knew that more than likely Ben had been at fault for Cathy disappearing. If he was dead in that house, Pickett had doubted their cold case would ever be solved unless he had left a note as to what had happened to Cathy.

Well, good old Ben did one better for them.

Pickett and Sarge got a warrant to go into Ben's home and they found him dead, as they expected, sitting in the chair in his basement.

And they also found Cathy.

Ben had dug up where she had been buried forty years before, just enough to see one of her mummified hands and some of her long blonde hair.

Then he had sat down in the chair facing her and stared at the grave until he died.

Pickett guessed that he had killed the woman he clearly loved.

Pickett figured it had been a crime of passion.

Sarge pretty much agreed.

Or as Sarge said, even more likely it had been an accident that he blamed himself for.

Turned out, at first glance as they dug her up, that she had a massive injury to the side of her head that more than likely had killed her. The injury looked like it could have been caused by hitting the corner of something.

The coroner who was digging her up had agreed that it looked that way on first blush.

Why Ben buried her and pretended to know nothing about her death would never be answered.

Sometimes a cold case was just easy to solve.

She and Sarge really hadn't had to do anything. Eventually someone would have gone in that house and stumbled on the same scene they found.

But besides the brother, there was no one left that she and Sarge could give closure to. And Cathy's disappearance had already destroyed the only surviving relative, her brother. He didn't seem to care that she had been found.

So they had been given an easy solution to a very old cold case, but unlike many other cases they solved, this one meant nothing to anyone.

They had found Cathy and no one cared.

And Pickett found that amazingly sad.

Someone should always care.

CHAPTER TWO

June 11th, 2017
Las Vegas, Nevada

Just as she did every morning, retired Detective Debra Pickett stood at the marble kitchen counter sipping on a cup of black coffee and watching as three cats chased each other around the living room and then back through the archway into what had been her condo before she and Sarge merged their two condos into one massive one.

It was amazing how fast the cats grew up. Just before Christmas, they had been kittens. Now, six months later they were all lanky, young adult, almost full-sized cats.

But still with the energy of kittens at times.

Nose, Pickett's black-and-white girl cat, couldn't get enough playing with Sarge's two orange tabbies, Pete and Ree. It was funny how Nose seemed to be in charge, acting above the two boys at times, and clearly controlling the games.

She was one smart little girl cat.

And the two orange boys were just sweethearts who purred at the slightest touch and loved to sit on laps when Picket and Sarge watched movies while Nose sat close.

And even as almost adults, the cats had more than enough room to play, considering that in the combined condos there were two kitchens, enough bedrooms to hold a small convention, and two full living rooms and dining rooms.

Pickett knew that having two penthouse condos connected was not how most retired Las Vegas detectives ended up. She was well-off financially from her divorce from the idiot who loved his secretary more than his money. But Sarge seemed to be at the next level of rich from money left to him by his parents.

As he had said one night, "Nothing to ever worry about."

Pickett sipped on her coffee again and watched the cat chase action as the three cats left the kitchen again at full speed, came back, and then disappeared up the stairs.

That was their normal trail and heaven help the human who crossed that trail during the "running of the cats," as Sarge called it.

As with every morning, she had gotten up and showered before Sarge and had made the coffee. They had no plans at all for the day, since they had solved the one case yesterday.

If you call what they did solving anything.

They had just been first onto an awful scene, nothing more.

So today they didn't even have a breakfast meeting with Robin, the third member of their team.

This morning Pickett wore jeans, a light-blue cotton blouse she left untucked, and tennis shoes. She had her badge in a holder on her belt covered by her blouse and her service gun in a holster under her arm. She would hide that with a very light, blue jacket when they went out.

The jacket was long-sleeved to keep her arms from being

burnt in the sun and she had a wide-brimmed hat to cover her head. She had such white skin, even the hint of sun often made her look like a cherry tomato. Amazing she had made it all these years in Las Vegas.

The weather today promised to be clear and hot. She could already see the heat shimmers coming off the buildings below their condo.

Sarge said he loved their routine of her going first in the morning and the fact that she never spent much time in the bathroom getting ready. His ex-wife, who had left him for another man, spent far too much time in the bathroom by Sarge's measure.

"Never could tell the difference if she took five minutes or an hour."

Pickett had socked him on the arm for that comment and told him, "Respect the work women do to look nice."

He had said he respected it, just didn't understand most of it.

Both of them had agreed that their marriages had been casualties of their jobs. It seemed that being a detective didn't leave much time and mental energy for making sure a marriage worked.

Sarge wasn't angry at his ex-wife, and said he even liked the guy she moved in with.

Sarge was far more forgiving than Pickett was with her ex-husband. Her ex deserved the young, blonde bimbo with massive bimbo-breasts, as she called them. Those two breasts had certainly cost the bastard a pretty penny in the settlement with Pickett.

More than enough to buy her condo, that was for sure.

Pickett looked at the empty countertop where they usually had the folders for their cases. She wished they had a case this morning. The Cold Poker Gang didn't meet for a few days yet, so they were case-less for the first time in a very long time. Felt damned odd, actually.

The Cold Poker Gang, made up of all retired detectives, met every week to play poker and talk cold cases. At this point, there were sixteen retired detectives in the gang, but only about ten to twelve showed up for the game on any given Tuesday. She and Sarge and Robin had decided they wouldn't miss a night.

And Sarge was the best player of the three of them, although Robin was getting better.

The poker and weekly conversations were fun, but what was the most important to Pickett was being able to carry her badge and gun again and feel useful, even after she had retired. Being a detective had been her identity and now, thanks to the Cold Poker Gang's special task-force status, she had that back.

She actually had been too young to retire, but the divorce had made her lose focus a few years back and question everything, including herself. Now she was barely over sixty and everyone said she looked younger. She felt younger, especially now that she was back working and living with Sarge.

Sarge said the sex helped with that and she certainly wasn't going to argue that point.

At that moment, Sarge came from down the hall, smiling at her. His hair still slightly wet from the shower as it was every morning.

He was the most handsome man she had ever met, she was sure of that. He had hazel eyes, thick gray hair, and a square jaw that gave him a superhero look at times, like he had been drawn right out of a comic book. This morning he was dressed in his normal jeans, dress shirt, and light jacket. He kept his badge where it always had been, on his belt on his right hip, and his gun in a carry holster under his arm.

Just as she did, he always put on a light jacket to cover the gun and the badge.

He kissed her, then picked up his coffee as the three cats, right on schedule, came tearing back down the stairs. This time the two orange cats were being chased by the black-and-white girl like she was herding them to their next part of the day.

As always, they stopped in the living room area and went to different chairs to take baths in the sun.

That was the end of the standard morning running of the cats. Now it was bath and then nap time.

Schedules. The cats lived by their schedules.

Sarge just shook his head and laughed at them, then sipped his coffee. After a moment he pointed to the empty kitchen counter. "Weird not having a case to work on."

"Very weird," Pickett said. "So what are we going to talk about over breakfast?"

"We may have to just sit and read the paper like normal old couples," he said, smiling.

"You calling me old?" she asked.

"That's going to take me a while to get out of isn't it?"

She laughed. "Buy me breakfast and I may let you live."

"Deal," he said.

CHAPTER THREE

June 11th, 2017
Las Vegas, Nevada

Sarge and Pickett had just gotten to their favorite table for breakfast in the Golden Nugget Buffet and Sarge was about to turn to the buffet when Robin showed up.

She was their third partner and Pickett's old partner from when they were both on the force. She topped the escalator and waved as she headed for the line to pay to get into the restaurant.

Sarge and Pickett had walked, as they did every morning, from their condo. The six-block walk from the Ogden had been nice, because it was early enough in the morning that the heat hadn't really set in yet.

Sarge had on a large cowboy-like hat that kept the sun off his face and a light jacket that covered his gun and badge. He liked the morning walks more than anything in his day, actually.

Gave him and Pickett a chance to really just be with each other and talk.

And get a little exercise.

Pickett had on a big floppy hat and also a light jacket that covered her gun and badge as well. They just looked like an eccentric older couple walking on Fremont Street as tourists. Sarge liked that they blended in so well, actually, without having to wear the stupid shorts and loud shirts of the real tourists.

The buffet was separated from the escalator area by a wall of plants and fake windows. The buffet was massive, with tables divided into three large sections. Everything was decorated in golden browns and brass tones that blended nicely with all the plants. The place made Sarge feel comfortable and he really liked starting his day off here with good food.

Tall, floor-to-ceiling windows let in a lot of light on the far side of the buffet. Those massive windows looked out over a large pool that seemed to always be jammed in the summer. Along the windows was the most popular area for tourists to sit in. He and Pickett always sat on the far side of the restaurant, away from the tourists and closer to the plant wall between them and the escalator.

Allowed them to talk quietly.

He and Pickett both waved to Robin and then they headed for the food.

He got started his normal morning three-egg, ham, and cheese omelet made fresh, then while that was being done, he got some fruit and a muffin from the pastry area.

He took the fruit back to the table. Robin was still in line to pay, so he went back and got a freshly made waffle, covered it with syrup, and then picked up his finished omelet.

He really was hungry today.

Actually, he had been eating like this more and more since

he and Pickett started working out down at the gym off of Sunset three evenings a week. They also used the Ogden gym room twice a week. He was feeling trimmer and leaner and often more hungry in the morning.

As he was sitting down, Robin finally got through the pay line and joined them.

Robin and Pickett, when active, had been known as the best detective team on the force. Sarge had heard of them far before he had gotten lucky enough to meet them after they retired. He couldn't believe his luck when he was assigned a Cold Poker Gang case with them.

The three of them had been working together ever since, and of course, he and Pickett were now living together.

Robin was solid, with shoulders like a weight-lifter, which she was not. She said those shoulders came naturally. She always dressed in a nice blouse and dress jacket that covered her badge and gun.

Her husband, Will, had the city's largest private security firm. He protected some of the most famous people in the world when they came to Vegas. And considering it was Vegas, he worked a lot. And Will and Robin were very, very rich.

"Scary rich," Pickett had told him one day.

Everyone in Las Vegas police trusted Will and his firm and his people. And the Chief of Police was one of Will's best friends.

Will and his people in his firm were amazingly good on computers and Robin was one of the best of them all. In the cold cases the three of them had worked together so far, he and Pickett had done the legwork while Robin did the computer work.

Sarge liked that arrangement. And it had solved some pretty

impossible cases for them. Cases that had sat cold in police files for decades.

When they were working cold cases, the three of them often met here for breakfast. Sarge had no idea why Robin was here today.

"Missed our pretty faces, huh?" Pickett said to Robin as Pickett came back to the table with her food from the buffet.

"Actually," Robin said, smiling, "I did. And you know the case we sort of wrapped yesterday?"

"Sort of wrapped?" Sarge asked, looking up from his waffle. He didn't like the sound of that at all.

"Cathy Wendt," Robin said, "more than likely killed by her boyfriend, Ben, forty years ago and buried in the basement."

"Thanks for bringing that image back up," Pickett said.

Robin smiled. "Glad I missed seeing it, but you two need to go back there to that house after breakfast."

Sarge looked at Robin, not really wanting an answer, but knowing he had to ask. "And why would we want to do that?"

"Because," Robin said, "They found two more blonde girls buried down there next to Cathy Wendt, if that was Cathy Wendt's body."

With a smile, Robin turned and headed to the buffet to get some breakfast.

"Oh, shit," Pickett said.

Sarge just stared at his food, shaking his head. The case had seemed so easy, so simply solved.

But nope.

He had a hunch this one was just getting started.

After all these years as a detective, you would think he would have learned that no crime was as simple as it seemed.

None.

CHAPTER FOUR

June 11ᵗʰ, 2017
Las Vegas, Nevada

Pickett and Sarge ate in silence, waiting for Robin to return with her food.

Pickett couldn't believe there had been more bodies down there in that unfinished basement. It seemed so logical that Ben had accidently killed his girlfriend and covered it up.

Open and shut.

But two more bodies showing up had certainly made that logical assumption a thing of the past.

Now they needed to know who all three of the other bodies were and why did Ben, if that was Ben, die in that chair, facing the bodies.

And did he kill Cathy or the other two?

Everything was now back in question.

Everything.

Robin came back with two plates of food and placed them in front of her spot at the table, then sat down.

"I see that little bombshell was a hit with the audience."

"Bombshell is right," Pickett said.

"Stink bomb," Sarge said.

Robin laughed.

"So how did you find out about this and what is going on?" Pickett asked, staring at her old partner as she started to eat.

"Got a call this morning from Cavanaugh," Robin said. "He got assigned the case, wants us back in."

Pickett liked Cavanaugh and always had, even from the days when they were on the force together. He was a great guy, standard square detective build and tall, although he had thinned a lot since he had gotten older. He had a mostly bald head and bright green eyes and was whip-smart. He always wore a sports coat that looked far too big for him. It seemed to be his trademark. Cavanaugh called it "early seventies sloppy."

"Thought Cavanaugh was set to retire and join the gang," Sarge said.

"First of July," Robin said. "He pulled this case because with new bodies, the chief needed to keep it active, but the chief wants us to stay on it, so he gave it to Cavanaugh, since he is almost part of the gang already, but still on active duty."

"Yeah, he still has to do the paperwork," Sarge said, laughing. "He so loves that."

"So what do we know," Pickett asked, "besides what we had in the Cathy Wendt cold file?"

"Not much more at all," Robin said. "They have removed the other two bodies and Cavanaugh wants to wait for you two before he does a search of that house. They will run tests on all three bodies, including DNA tests, to see if they can figure out who those three are."

Pickett sort of sat back. "So none of them may be Cathy Wendt."

"We assumed it was because it being Ben's house," Robin said, "and the blonde hair, but there is a chance that Cathy may not be there. Chief has given permission to put a rush on a preliminary DNA test and two detectives this morning got a DNA sample from Cathy's brother."

"A rush on a cold case?" Sarge asked, clearly as surprised as Pickett felt.

"This isn't really a cold case anymore," Robin said. "A mass grave was found, so that warrants some extra."

"Are they still digging down there?" Pickett asked, afraid of the answer.

"They are," Robin said. "But the ground-penetrating radar doesn't show any more bodies."

"We can only hope it ends with three," Sarge said.

Robin agreed with that.

Pickett remembered what Robin had said about all three being blonde. That had to be important in some way, but damned if Pickett, after making such a bad assumption yesterday, wanted to even try to guess what that was about.

"Are the fine folks doing the digging going to have any idea how long those girls have been down there?" Sarge asked.

"They will get it close," Robin said. "Between the evidence in the holes like clothing and identification, we hope, and the autopsy, it should be within six months."

"That will help," Pickett said.

Robin nodded. "I already have a computer search running of girls with blonde hair that went missing before and after Cathy Wendt. It should be done by the time I get home and you get back to the house with Cavanaugh."

Pickett nodded and the three of them sat silently eating as

the background noise of a busy Las Vegas buffet swirled around them. They just didn't have enough information yet to figure out which way to even start. Pickett had a hunch they might find some sort of trail at Ben's house in the search.

But until then, all three of them were just not speculating.

Finally, as they all finished, Sarge said simply, "Stink bomb. This case is a stink bomb."

Pickett and Robin both nodded.

Pickett agreed completely.

Everything about this case smelled off and seemed off.

And she had a hunch they were only getting started.

CHAPTER FIVE

June 11th, 2017
Las Vegas, Nevada

Cavanaugh's unmarked black sedan was parked in front of the rundown old house. A police medical van sat in the driveway in front of Ben's old car and two other police cars were parked on either side.

Ben's carport that covered his old car had been taped off as a crime scene area, as well as the rest of the backyard.

Sarge and Pickett climbed out into the heat and both took their light jackets off and tossed them into the back seat of Pickett's Jeep Grand Cherokee before heading inside. There was no doubt that house was going to be hot. It had been hot yesterday when they first went in, and now, with the doors open, it was going to be cooking in there by noon.

Luckily, a thin haze in the sky kept the sun from pounding down too hard and the day was only forecast to hit just over ninety.

They signed in with the officer at the door. It had been a while since either of them had actually been on an active crime scene. Cold cases didn't tend to bring up active crime scenes that often.

The inside of the house looked like it had frozen in time in the mid-seventies. Old brown couches that looked like they might not support a person lined both sides of the living room. A large-screen television was on a stand on one wall and a newer, but worn recliner faced it.

There were knickknacks and pictures on the shelves on one wall and the floor was covered with a brown-stained carpet that looked, before it had a lot of wear, like it used to be shag.

The odor was of dry and rot and dust. Mostly dust.

The house inside was the same temperature as outside at the moment, which was warm, but not hot.

Sarge wondered if he and Pickett should get some masks if they started moving things around to guard against the dust.

At that moment Cavanaugh came in from the direction of the kitchen and the basement door. He was wearing just his dress shirt and slacks with a badge on his belt and a gun under his arm in a holster. Somewhere his large jacket had found a resting place.

He was also wearing a white breathing mask over his mouth and nose and white, soiled evidence gloves.

He pulled the mask to one side as he entered, smiled, and said, "You two just couldn't wait one more month before uncovering a pile of shit for me, could you?"

"We wanted you to enjoy your last month," Pickett said, going to him and hugging him.

Sarge waited until Pickett was done molesting the poor cop, then shook his hand.

Then Sarge said, "Hell, the paperwork on this alone is going to keep you busy for a month."

"Oh, god, don't remind me," Cavanaugh said. "Just the paperwork against an unknown estate to get a search warrant for this place this morning took almost an hour."

"Who is Ben's heir?" Pickett asked.

Cavanaugh only shrugged. "The title on the house says Ben March, but got a hunch that's as phony as they come."

"I'll get Robin on it," Pickett said.

"Thanks," Cavanaugh said. "Might save us all some grief down the road if we knew who really owned this place now."

Sarge watched as she quickly texted Robin the questions "Ben…heir??? And who really owns this house???"

"So," Sarge asked, "not finding any more bodies buried down there?"

"Three is more than enough," Cavanaugh said.

"So what are you thinking we should do, detective?" Pickett asked Cavanaugh, looking around.

"Grab a mask and a couple flashlights off the kitchen counter," Cavanaugh said, "put on some gloves, and each take a room. See if we can find anything that would give us a hint as to what happened in this horror house. Three bedrooms and a bath down the hall. Kitchen, dining, living area here. Back porch and the carport and a tool shed. I'll deal with searching the basement around the crime scene there and then work my way back up into the kitchen."

Sarge liked that idea. He had no desire to go back down into that basement.

"All right if we open blinds and windows to get more light and some air flow?" Sarge asked.

"Be my guest," Cavanaugh said. "Never saw anything in that search warrant that said we have to treat this like a damned cave. But forensics won't be here to go over everything until later this afternoon."

Sarge laughed. He really liked Cavanaugh and it was going to be great having him with the Cold Poker Gang.

A minute later Sarge and Pickett, breathing masks in place, gloves on, went down the hall to the two bedrooms on the end.

"Let's get the windows opened first," Sarge said, so they both went into the bedroom on the left. The room was dark and just to get across it they had to use a flashlight.

Two windows facing out over the backyard were there, side-by-side. A double bed was against the wall on the other side and a sliding closet door covered part of a third wall.

They carefully got the blinds open without stirring up too much dust, then managed to get both windows pushed up about halfway before the windows stuck.

At least the room was now bathed in light, showing off the swirling dust they did stir up. And there was a slight breeze going through the room and down the hall toward the open front door. Anything would help.

They went across the hall and pushed open the door there. Two windows looked out over the front yard and street.

They did the same, getting both windows open first so they could see the room, and the cross breeze between the two rooms increased.

Then when Sarge turned around to look at the room, he almost choked.

And beside him, Pickett gasped.

One full wall was covered in Polaroid pictures of a blonde girl. A large bed faced the picture wall.

From the one picture they had seen of Cathy Wendt from the file when she disappeared, Sarge would bet that all those pictures were of her.

There were hundreds of pictures on that wall, all clearly old, many yellowing as old Polaroid pictures tended to do. Most of the pictures were nude shots of a smiling, laughing young blonde.

"I think I'll let you take this room," Sarge said, starting for the door.

"No chance in hell, mister," Pickett said. "We do this room together."

Sarge stopped and laughed, then looked back at the wall of old pictures, some of them curling. A few had come off the pins on the wall and dropped to the floor. Clearly Ben and Cathy had been having a lot of fun before she died.

"And just when I thought this house couldn't get any creepier," Sarge said.

"Don't challenge it," Pickett said.

She had a real good point about that.

CHAPTER SIX

June 11th, 2017
Las Vegas, Nevada

They found more shoeboxes of pictures of Cathy Wendt in the top of the closet. Most of them were of her clothed and in school or at a party or in a car. Some of them showed Cathy and who Pickett assumed was Ben together, laughing.

Cathy looked very young, from what Pickett could tell.

Pickett would check to make sure that really was Ben in those photos. As if they knew what Ben actually looked like.

She shook her head at that thought. No more assumptions with this case. A couple photos were of a meal with Cathy, what appeared to be her mother and young brother, and Ben. Pickett had no idea who took the picture.

It was clear that Ben had taken all the nude pictures of Cathy, right here in the same room. Only this room looked to have been his parents' bedroom.

That made no sense at all.

None.

And felt very creepy, actually.

"Very little left here from his parents," Sarge said, after they had searched for a while. "But I am thinking this was their room."

Pickett nodded. "I agree. I think it was as well. I'll text Robin to look into Ben's parents. We have no idea on anything here."

She quickly sent Robin a text that said, "Check out Ben's parents. Wish you were here."

Robin wrote back almost instantly. "Will do. Glad you are having fun."

Pickett quickly snapped a few pictures of the wall of nude photos and sent them to Robin with a message, "See if this is actually Cathy Wendt from the missing person's file."

Robin wrote back simply, "Yuck."

It took Pickett and Sarge a good hour to slowly work through all the stuff in the closet, spreading much of it out on the bed and piling some old clothes on the floor after they checked the pockets.

They all appeared to be a man's clothes.

Then they checked the chest of drawers and through all the clothes in there, pulling out the drawers and looking at the bottoms of the drawers for anything taped there.

Nothing.

They even got down on both sides of the bed and inspected everything under the bed and then along behind the drapes.

More nothing.

Only the pictures, the furniture, and men's clothing.

So finally they went back out to the kitchen to take a break, get some water, and change out their masks and gloves.

Sarge's face was covered in black streaks from the sweat and the dust and she knew her face was as well.

The house was slowly starting to heat up. Another couple of hours would make it into an oven, even with the windows opened.

At that moment Cavanaugh came back up from the basement and took off his mask, looking just as dirty and sweaty as Pickett felt.

"Any luck?" he asked.

"Not sure if you would call it luck," Pickett said. "We spent the last hour on the room on the right, both of us. Go take a look at the wall in there and you'll see why."

Cavanaugh walked down the hallway and into the bedroom.

Then about thirty seconds later he came back, shaking his head.

"No clue what that means," Pickett said.

"With luck, just kids in love enjoying sex," Cavanaugh said.

Sarge nodded to that. "The 1970s equivalent of sexting."

"But in his parent's bedroom?" Pickett asked.

"You think that was their bedroom?" Cavanaugh asked.

Both Pickett and Sarge nodded.

"Okay, from fun play to a little kinky," Cavanaugh said, shaking his head.

After a ten-minute break and a full bottle of water each, the three went their opposite directions. Pickett was really glad she didn't have to go back in that basement as Cavanaugh was doing.

She and Sarge did a complete search of the first bedroom they had opened up. Nothing at all and it didn't look like the room had been used much at all.

Then they went back to the third bedroom that was on the left across the hall from the house's only bathroom.

They opened the door to pitch blackness and a very dry smell of age and dust. This room had been closed up even longer than the other two. Even with the door open you could only see the outline of a bed and a dresser.

Pickett shined her flashlight toward the blinds and she and Sarge got the blinds opened slowly to hold down the dust and then opened the window to let the room air some.

When she turned around, the sight shoved her backwards right into Sarge.

The room, on all three walls, was covered in naked Polaroid photos of what appeared to be three different blonde girls. A different girl on each wall.

All of them sort of looked like Cathy, but were not Cathy.

And in the bed, on one side of the bed, covered up to her chin, was yet another dead blonde girl. Her skin mummified and dried, her eyes empty sockets. The blankets barely showed a dent where her mummified body lay.

She clearly had been in that bed and dead a very, very long time since her hair had fallen off her head onto the pillow.

"I'm really starting to hate this place," Sarge said, reaching out and taking Pickett's hand.

Carefully, making sure to not touch anything in the room even with their gloves on, they went back out and to the kitchen.

Pickett called down the stairs to Cavanaugh.

"First bedroom on the left," Pickett said when he showed up in the kitchen. Both she and Sarge had taken off their masks and gloves and were both drinking water.

Cavanaugh looked worried. He pulled his mask aside and went down the hallway.

"Son of a bitch" echoed up the hallway and into the kitchen.

When he came back down the hall he actually looked angry.

"We'll meet you here early tomorrow morning," Pickett said. "To continue the search."

"Thanks," Cavanaugh said, nodding as he pulled out his cell

phone. "I can hardly wait to see what you two will find then. There might be bodies under the carpet for all we know."

Sarge and Pickett both laughed.

Sarge patted Cavanaugh on the back and then Sarge and Pickett got out of that place and into the cool air-conditioning of her car.

She had seen a lot of very strange and horrific things over her years as a detective. That bedroom ranked right up there near the top of the list.

Twenty minutes later they were naked, standing in their large shower together, trying to get the dust and grime and memory of that house of horrors off of each other.

PART TWO

Bigger and Bigger

CHAPTER SEVEN

June 11th, 2017
Las Vegas, Nevada

Sarge had suggested that they head out for lunch after their shower and a change of clothes. Pickett had called Robin and they had decided to meet at the Bellagio Café.

He just needed to be around some live people, some reasonably sane people, even though they were Las Vegas tourists. The image of that long-dead girl in that bed surrounded by naked photos of three young girls had rocked him.

Something horrid had happened in that house a long time ago. And not a bit of it made any sense at all. When they had first thought it was just a boyfriend accidentally killing his girlfriend and covering it up, that was logical.

But three more girls' bodies, all looking like Cathy Wendt, made no sense at all.

So getting out to a normal place, having some good food,

and trying to make sense out of it all with Robin and Pickett appealed to him.

Pickett got them to the valet parking at the Bellagio in only twenty minutes. The day had turned hot, but thankfully, they had to only be in the heat this time from the car to the casino front door.

The Bellagio Café was the casino's main twenty-four-hour restaurant, designed to comfortably seat hundreds at a time if needed. It had nice wood tables and booths separated from each other by rows of plants. Their favorite booth was in the back, surrounded on three sides by plants and against the back wall.

From there they could see the entire restaurant, have private conversations, and the laughing and bells from the casino floor were only a background noise.

They were already seated and had ordered two iced teas and three glasses of water when Robin wound her way through the tables and joined them. She was wearing her normal jeans, light blouse, and light jacket that covered her badge and gun. She was carrying a thin folder with some paper in it.

All three of them pretty much dressed the same in the summer.

"Cavanaugh filled me in and sent me some pictures," Robin said as she dropped into the booth and took a long drink of her water.

"Nasty, huh?"

Robin nodded. "Original police search missed the body because of the lack of electricity. They just opened the door, saw a dark bedroom, and closed it. Cavanaugh feels bad that you two had to find that."

Sarge laughed. "No he doesn't."

Robin smiled. "He wanted me to say that because he hopes

you two will come back in the morning, early, before it gets hot, and keep searching."

Pickett laughed. "Kind of him to think of us. We told him we would see him in the morning."

"He said after finding that horror show," Robin said, "he wouldn't blame you if you didn't show."

"We'll be there," Sarge said.

"I told him that, too," Robin said.

At that moment a waiter came up, took their order, and left. All three of them were here so often, they didn't even need to look at the menus. Sarge kind of liked that about coming here. Made him feel like this place was sort of an extension of his home, and in a way it was. Just as the Golden Nugget Buffet was for breakfast.

"So did you find anything?" Pickett asked Robin.

"Parents are coming up as very strange," Robin said. "The Ben that owns that house has no heirs as far as I can find, assuming that is the Cathy Wendt Ben that was in that chair."

"Can't assume anything on this anymore," Pickett said.

Sarge agreed with that completely.

"The parents of the Ben that owned that place seemed to have existed, sort of, from what I can tell from the 1970s and sketchy records. But I am getting the sense they were all falsified records. Back then that sort of stuff could be bought."

"You thinking Ben lived in that house alone," Sarge asked, stunned, "back in high school?"

"My guess is Ben was a lot older than we thought he was," Robin said. "We won't know for sure until they get done with the body at the medical examiner's office. But records show that his parents bought the house with cash."

"So there is a theory that he lived there," Pickett said, "set up phony parents, enrolled in high school."

Robin nodded.

Sarge wasn't buying it. "Why would you jump to that conclusion on this? I know taking those pictures of Cathy Wendt in his parents' bedroom was creepy, but that wouldn't lead to that kind of jump."

"Agreed," Robin said. "But here is what I have found so far from records that have been put online." She pulled a few sheets of paper out of her notebook and handed one to Sarge.

It was a high school list of students from 1977.

"I went to high school records first. Ben March is listed as a junior with Cathy Wendt."

Sarge spotted the names and nodded and handed the list to Pickett.

"The address of the house you found is in that school district. So as a lark I went to a second high school on the other side of town. Ben April is registered there as a junior the next year, a transfer in from Utah."

Sarge was getting a sinking feeling where this was headed and he didn't like it at all.

"Did a blonde girl go missing from that class in 1978?" Pickett asked.

"One did," Robin said, nodding. "I'm still culling out all the missing blonde girls I found from surrounding years and expanding the search a little."

"Damn it," Sarge said.

"I have a computer program running," Robin said, "doing more searches of other high schools in the area and in all of Nevada that correspond with a Ben being registered and a blonde classmate going missing. I'll know more after I get back from lunch."

"How did he register in another high school while his house was across the city?" Pickett asked.

"Don't say it," Sarge said, holding up his hand to Robin. "Just don't say it."

Robin laughed. "Ben April lived with his mother and father, who seem fake as well, in a home near the high school. The house is still in Ben April's name."

At that moment Sarge's bacon club sandwich arrived and even though it looked and smelled wonderful, he no longer was sure he was hungry.

CHAPTER EIGHT

June 11th, 2017
Las Vegas, Nevada

Pickett was stunned at the pattern that was developing from just a little research from Robin. Robin was fairly convinced that a young guy by the name of Ben had registered in at least seven high schools from 1975 through 1982 as a junior. He had just used the month as his last name, starting with January and going through August.

From what little bit Robin had found, he was always a transfer in his junior year from another state. And for the April name, she had found the house that he had lived in.

They decided that after lunch Pickett and Sarge would swing by the April place, see if it was occupied, before ruining Cavanaugh's day with needing yet another search warrant.

But they still had so many questions.

Assuming Cathy Wendt was one of the bodies found in the

house, which as far as Pickett was concerned was now a huge assumption, who were the other three?

From the other high schools, maybe?

Robin had a lot more research to do and she was pulling in one of Will's top computer people to help her, since so much of the stuff she needed was so dated.

And Robin was expanding her research to the University of Nevada as well.

Pickett had no doubt that at some point she and Sarge would be digging through old paper records. When you had crimes that were forty years old, that was the nature of the beast.

So after lunch, she and Sarge, with her driving her Jeep Grand Cherokee, headed for the second home that Ben March, or April, or whatever his real name was, had owned.

The place was small, as was the first house, in an old neighborhood that had seen much better days. It had been painted white at one time, but now looked a dirty gray. The house had no lawn and nothing but weeds surrounding it. An old, faded blue Toyota with two flat tires was in the carport.

Trash littered the driveway to the house and it was clear no one had lived there for a very long time. Sadly, it was not the only house on the street that looked like that. Not even close.

They sat in the car and stared at the place. Finally Picket asked, "Want to even try to see if anyone's home?"

She really didn't want to get out into the heat to even walk around the place.

"I suppose we better before bothering Cavanaugh," Sarge said.

Pickett agreed, but she had a hunch it would be a worthless venture.

They both made sure their guns were in place and their jackets covering them before they climbed out.

The hot air hit them like a hammer, not at all comforting. More oppressive.

A faded notice from the power company had the power turned off a long, long time ago. They wandered into the back through the carport. The only tracks in the dirt were of cats and dogs.

No human tracks.

The backyard was full of trash and overgrown with dried weeds.

Most of the other homes she could see on both sides had similar backyards. One spark would level this neighborhood, of that there was no doubt.

They stood in the shade of the carport and Sarge called Cavanaugh.

"Got another problem for you," he said.

He listened for a moment and then laughed.

"No, Robin found another home that Ben owned that looks like the one you are in. Power off, no one lived here for year or more at least."

He listened and then again laughed.

"Want us to wait for you here? We are standing beside the house now."

He nodded and gave Cavanaugh the exact address for the warrant.

After a moment Sarge nodded. "What do you want us to order for you?"

Sarge nodded, then said, "See you there."

He hung up and turned to Pickett. "We're meeting him at the Burger King two blocks from here. The poor guy hasn't had lunch yet."

Pickett smiled and asked as they headed for her car, "Don't you miss all the details of being on active duty?"

Sarge shook his head. "Not a bit. Being on this task force is heaven. We get to be detectives and not do any of the paperwork. And I got a hunch this case is going to have paperwork."

"A ton of it, even if we don't find anything strange in this place." Which she was sure wouldn't be the case.

They got back in the car and Pickett got the air-conditioning going. Then for a moment they sat and looked at the house sitting in the heat.

"I don't have a good feeling about that place," she said.

"Neither do I," Sarge said.

Pickett stared at the house and then shuddered. "You get the sense we are finding an old serial killer's graveyards?"

"And each house is like a tombstone?" Sarge said. "Yeah, thought of that. Creepy."

"I think, from the looks of the pictures on the walls," Pickett said, "each place is more of a memorial."

"Serial killers like to take trophies," Sarge said. "The photos, the bodies, all could be that."

"But why keep a body in a bed and bury the other three?" Pickett asked.

"Real kinky," Sarge said.

Pickett laughed and then said, "More than likely that was the case."

But more than likely, there was a lot more to this than they were finding so far.

And that worried her more than she wanted to admit.

How much more could there be?

She knew the answer was a great deal.

CHAPTER NINE

June 11th, 2017
Las Vegas, Nevada

The air-conditioning inside the Burger King was working overtime, so the place had an arctic feel to it. They had already ordered and found a plastic booth away from others.

Sarge didn't miss needing to grab food like this while on the go on a case. One thing he loved about being on the Cold Poker Gang task force was that they set their own pace. Cold cases seldom needed to be done quickly.

Cavanaugh came in, waved at them, and headed for the bathroom. Sarge could see that he was covered in dust and dirt.

They had just gotten their orders. Both he and Pickett had gotten two bottles of water and a milkshake each. They had bought Cavanaugh a Whopper with fries and a diet Coke and a bottle of water for later.

It took Cavanaugh a minute to emerge from the restroom, his face red from splashing cold water on it, his hair wet. But he was smiling. Water had dripped down the front of his large suit jacket and he didn't even seem to care.

"Wow, that felt good," he said.

Sarge shoved the tray with the food toward him and Cavanaugh nodded, took a long drink of the Coke, then dug into the wonderful-smelling fries.

"Get the new victim out of the bed?" Pickett asked.

Cavanaugh nodded. "Looked to be about the same age and height and such as the ones in the ground downstairs. Identification on all of them is going to take a little time, but the chief, with this fourth body, has put a priority on it in the labs. And we are all forbidden to talk to the press. So far, thankfully, no one has caught wind of this."

"What is the press?" Pickett asked, trying to be serious.

Cavanaugh laughed. "One more damn month and I can be on that side of that question."

So as he ate, they filled him in on Robin's research so far and how she had found this house and how she was searching missing person's reports and so on.

"Thanks for doing a drive-by before I went after a warrant," he said as he finished his hamburger and went back to work on what was left of the fries.

He took out his phone, checked something, then said, "We just got the warrant, so we're set to go take a look."

"Oh, joy," Pickett said.

Sarge laughed, then said, "Hang on."

He stood and went to the counter, got a glass for ice water, filled it half full of ice and then water and went back to the table with a pile of napkins.

"Put this on your neck," Sarge said to Cavanaugh as he opened a few napkins to their full length, combined them and dipped them in the ice water. "We don't want you heat-stroking out on us before you join the gang."

"After I join will be fine?" Cavanaugh asked, smiling as he did what Sarge suggested.

"Oh, we won't care then," Pickett said. "We're all old, remember?"

Cavanaugh laughed and said thanks. Then asked how much he owed for the lunch and Sarge waved it off.

Then he and Pickett both put the iced-napkins on their necks and Sarge filled the glass with ice and water again and took a bunch more napkins and they headed out into the heat and the second house, each carrying bottles of water.

The iced-napkins on the neck was an old trick Sarge had learned a long time ago to help with the heat. He had a hunch they were going to need it today.

Pickett parked in front of the place and Cavanaugh pulled his sedan into the driveway behind the old car in the carport.

Cavanaugh gave them gloves and flashlights and they redid their iced-napkins on their necks. Cavanaugh had called in to the local cops what they were doing and a patrol car would join them shortly.

Then with Cavanaugh carrying a crowbar, they headed around back. No point in opening up the front door.

Cavanaugh first pounded on the door and yelled, "Police."

Then he cranked the door open quickly with his shoulder and the crowbar, pushing it in hard. It broke off some rotted trim on the door.

Sarge was impressed. Cavanaugh looked big and wore a sloppy coat, but clearly the guy had kept himself in good shape as well.

Inside was pitch dark and smelled of dust and old air.

"Before we open the place up, let's do a quick search with

the flashlights," Cavanaugh said. "Got any idea if there is a basement?"

"Robin said there was from the house plans she looked up," Pickett said.

"Shit," Cavanaugh said. "I'll take it. You two have fun with the bedrooms again."

"Thanks," Sarge said. "I think."

Then together, he and Pickett started down the dark hallway.

It was the last place Sarge had ever wanted to be on a bright, hot June day.

The very last.

CHAPTER TEN

June 11th, 2017
Las Vegas, Nevada

Pickett instantly hated this place. The house had the exact same layout as Ben's other home, if this actually was one of his houses. There had to have been thousands of these small three-bedroom homes built around Las Vegas in the 1960s and early 1970s.

Three bedrooms and a bath down a hall, a living room on the front half, a kitchen and small dining room on the back half. They had come into the small dining room area and there was a Formica-top table with four chairs, all pushed in under the table.

The kitchen counter was Formica as well and covered in dirt. Some really old dishes filled the sink, all crusted.

The door to the basement was off the dining room on the right of the back door.

Cavanaugh went slowly down those stairs as she and Sarge headed through the edge of the kitchen and down the hallway.

It felt as if they were almost under black water once they got away from the light coming in from the back door, with dust-motes floating in the air around them in the beams of their flashlights.

Picket could almost hear her own breathing.

"Start in the bedroom on the left," Sarge said.

"Okay," Pickett said.

All three bedroom doors were closed, so they opened up the door on the left at the end of the hallway.

"Damn it all to hell," Sarge said as he panned his light on the mummified remains of a blonde girl in the bed.

The poor girl had to have been dead for decades from the look of it.

Picket just wanted to be sick. This one looked exactly like the one in the other house. Blankets pulled up to her chin, blonde hair fallen around her head on the pillow.

How was this even possible that none of these girls had been found? Decades clearly had passed. Just the smell of a rotting corpse in a neighbor's house should have alerted someone all those years ago.

She and Sarge put their lights on the walls and the walls were covered with Polaroid images of at least two, if not more, young teenage blonde girls, all naked and smiling, clearly having fun.

And all of them seemed to be in a bedroom like the parents' bedroom at the other house.

There was no stress at all in the girls being photographed without clothes on. They were clearly enjoying themselves and in some pictures mugging for the camera.

Pickett left the room and Sarge pulled the door closed behind them.

The door on the right had an empty bed, thank heavens, but

again the walls were covered with hundreds of Polaroid pictures of naked blonde girls.

"How in the world did this guy get so many young girls to take their clothes off for him?" Sarge asked. "And look happy doing so?"

"That might be the question that gives us some answers," Pickett said. But right now she had no idea either.

They again closed the door, then went to the bedroom across the hall from the bathroom.

Inside were more pictures on the wall and two blonde girls in the bed. Same scene, both with covers pulled up under their chins, both mummified.

Impossible.

Pickett couldn't believe they were finding this.

Just impossible.

They backed out of the room and pulled the door closed, then went back to the kitchen with the light coming in through the open back door. It was everything Pickett could do to not just go on out into the heat and sun.

Cavanaugh was just coming up the stairs.

"Anything?" Sarge asked.

"Gravel and dirt floor," Cavanaugh said, "and an old wooden rocking chair facing the open area like in the other house."

"So more than likely some bodies down there," Sarge said.

All Pickett could do was shake her head. She was numb. She remembered that feeling from horrid cases when she was on active duty.

Cavanaugh just nodded.

"We got three bodies up here," Pickett said.

"Three?" Cavanaugh asked.

"All mummified like the one in the other house," Sarge said.

"Decades old at least. One in the back left bedroom and two in the bedroom across from the bathroom."

"And naked pictures of young blonde girls on all the walls of all three bedrooms," Pickett said.

Cavanaugh took a deep breath of the musty air, then started down the hallway to take a look.

"We'll be in my car," Pickett said.

"I'll be right out," Cavanaugh said, not turning around.

Sarge let Pickett lead back to the car and then get the air-conditioning running.

Then about five minutes later, Cavanaugh came out, walking slowly, clearly thinking.

He came over and climbed into the back seat and Pickett handed him a bottle of cold water they had brought from Burger King.

Cavanaugh downed about half of it.

"This has sure become a mess," Cavanaugh said. "Hang on and let me call the chief and see how he wants us to deal with this."

Pickett turned in the seat to face Cavanaugh in the back seat while he got in touch with the Las Vegas Chief of Police.

"The second house has bodies as well," Cavanaugh said. "Three upstairs, a chance of more buried in the basement. The bodies are as old as the first one. Mummified after decades."

He listened for a minute, then said, "Just me and Sarge and Pickett. Robin was the one who found the house, and she and her people with Will are still working on this. There might be more houses."

Again Cavanaugh paused to listen to something the chief was saying. Then he said, "We're sitting in her car out front right now."

"Understood, sir," Cavanaugh said and hung up his phone and held it in his hand.

"Well?" Sarge said. "The Gang shoved down the road on this yet?"

Cavanaugh laughed. "No chance you are going to get that lucky. Can you two meet me at around 8 at the first house tomorrow? We'll finish searching there and then come over here to see what we can find. The tech folks should be mostly done, except down in the basement, by then."

Pickett glanced at Sarge and he nodded.

"See you in the morning," Pickett said.

Cavanaugh started to get out, but Sarge said, "Hang on."

He made the active detective another ice-water pack for the back of his neck.

Cavanaugh put it on and said, "Thanks!"

Then he closed the door and headed to his own car, his phone against his ear.

"Have I said lately how happy I am that I am no longer active?" Sarge said.

Pickett laughed as she pulled away. "I think I've said it more."

And she honestly was very glad she didn't have to have the afternoon and evening Cavanaugh was about to have.

CHAPTER ELEVEN

June 12th, 2017
Las Vegas, Nevada

Sarge had slept hard and was still feeling it as he headed down the hall from their bedroom and into the kitchen. Just at that moment, their three cats flashed past him and headed up the stairs.

"Almost died right there," he said, laughing, as the cats vanished from sight.

Pickett handed him a cup of coffee and kissed him. "Death by cat stampede. Everyone who has owned cats would know exactly what happened."

Sarge nodded and sipped on his morning coffee, trying to clear his mind for the day ahead.

The sun wasn't really even up yet, but the sky was colored with what promised to be a beautiful sunrise.

Yesterday afternoon they had gotten back from the second house after calling Robin and telling her what they had found, taken another shower, taken naps with the cats. Then he had cooked Pickett and himself a light dinner and they had watched a movie while sharing a large tub of popcorn.

Both of them fell asleep in the middle of the movie. He didn't have much memory of how they made it to bed.

Robin was going to meet them for breakfast this morning at the Golden Nugget Buffet, even though it was earlier than they normally got there. More than likely she had more stuff to share with them, but unlike most cases, on this one he wasn't sure if he actually wanted to know.

So far they had seven known bodies of young girls, all killed decades ago by some means not even certain yet. He had no doubt the body count was going to go higher.

He got a cooler out of the pantry and filled it with ice and then bottles of water from the fridge. Then he put three cold packs in the ice as well to use for their necks instead of using napkins, which dried out quickly and fell apart.

They drove to the Golden Nugget parking garage and made it up to the buffet in about the same amount of time as it would have taken them to walk. But this way they could leave directly from breakfast to head back to the first house to meet Cavanaugh.

Robin was already eating and the buffet had a slightly different feel about it because it was an hour earlier. This tourist crowd seemed to be in a little more of a hurry. More than likely to catch a plane or something.

And the big windows that usually streamed in sun were much darker. That changed the mood a little as well.

Robin had her carry bag next to her with her laptop and notebooks in it.

They waved at her as they headed to the buffet to get food.

Sarge stayed with his normal omelet and waffle and fruit.

After he and Pickett were both eating and Robin had finished, she brought up her notebook.

"How many more houses?" Sarge asked, deciding to get right to the point.

"Four more," Robin said, "for the high school years. All owned by fake parents and paid in cash for, all in bad neighborhoods."

"All still in his name, or fake name?" Pickett asked.

Robin nodded. "All had their power turned off about the same time a year ago for non-payment."

Sarge forced himself to keep eating. He had known the body count was going to go up. Now the question was how high.

"I'm hearing a lot left out," Pickett said, looking at Robin.

Sarge looked up as Robin nodded. He had never seen her so upset and tired-looking.

"I've been trying to track his money," Robin said. "Money is one of the only things that pretended to have a computer trail back then, so I figured I could help there."

"And…?" Pickett asked.

"I traced it all the way to 1975," Robin said. "When he first took the name Ben January and came into town and enrolled in high school, he was actually twenty-three years old, but looked much younger."

"You find his real name?"

"Benjamin Ronald States," she said, nodding.

That surprised Sarge. Robin was good, but how had she done that so fast?

"Originally from New York," Robin said. "Parents killed when he was seventeen and a junior in high school. He was an only child and his parents were very rich."

Sarge watched as Robin pulled out some notes. "He was

dating a blonde girl by the name of Mindy when his parents died. She dropped him."

"Lost his parents, lost his girlfriend," Sarge said. "Ugly."

"How did you find all this out?" Pickett asked.

"Yeah, I am stunned," Sarge said.

Robin beamed. "Extreme high-tech facial recognition that Will uses for security, combined with high school yearbooks that are online. I wrote a program to scan all high school yearbooks for Ben, cutting down the points of similarity. Found three hundred on the first pass, then actually did a full facial recognition scan of those three hundred and got him. Took some high-speed processing and about six hours. Once I found him, I made a couple phone calls to old classmates."

Sarge was very glad all this technology was on the side of good at this point.

"Brilliant," Pickett said.

"Thanks," she said, smiling.

"So did he have a house here under his real name?" Sarge asked.

"He does," Robin said. "A beautiful mansion out to the north of town on a ridge. He owed a land development firm for the last thirty years and made himself even richer than he was when he got here. His hobby was nude photography. In fact, over the last three decades he has won awards for his nudes and his pictures are shown in galleries all over the country. He's that good."

Sarge just nodded and pushed his plate away. Pieces were coming together thanks to Robin, but they still had so many unanswered question.

And they still had five houses, more than likely with bodies in them.

"One thing I find interesting," Robin said. "There are no houses for January and February. March was the first one."

"One more thing," Robin said. "Benjamin Ronald States was married, still is married, for the last thirty-eight years, to a woman whose maiden name was Cathy Wendt."

"Still is married?" Sarge asked. He must have heard Robin wrong.

Robin nodded. "They are both still alive."

All Sarge and Pickett could do was just stare at Robin.

And Sarge knew instantly, from the look on Robin's face, that she wasn't kidding.

CHAPTER TWELVE

June 12th, 2017
Las Vegas, Nevada

Pickett damned near fell over backward when Robin said that Ben and Cathy were still alive. How in the world could Cathy Wendt still be alive? And if this Benjamin Ronald States was the same Ben, what in the world was going on?

"Are you sure?"

Robin nodded. "But remember, I tracked him from his pictures, so there is a chance I am wrong on this."

Pickett nodded, reminding herself that there could be no assumptions.

"So now what do we do?" Sarge asked.

"We tell Cavanaugh," Pickett said. "This is an active case, so we tell him what we have found and get some police watching that Ben as we dig for evidence to put the guy away, if he really did all this."

"My gut tells me he didn't," Robin said. "Something is still off on the money trail and those six houses. I'll keep digging."

"And if Ben from the Cathy Wendt case is still alive," Sarge said, "who the hell was in that rocking chair in the basement?"

"And who are all the girls," Pickett asked, "both the dead ones and the ones in the pictures?"

Only the sounds of the early morning customers in the buffet answered those questions.

At that moment Robin's phone beeped and she said, "Cavanaugh."

"Morning, Detective," she said. "I'm with Pickett and Sarge and they are about to head your way."

She listened for a moment, then sat back, clearly stunned.

"I'll tell them, and they have some news for you as well when they see you."

She laughed, then said, "Sorry, but yes, more houses."

She nodded. "They will see you soon."

She hung up and smiled. "He hasn't had his first cup of coffee yet."

Pickett smiled. No detective after a long night should ever be talked to before a first cup of coffee.

"So what shocked you?" Sarge said.

"He called to tell me that all four bodies at the March house had been embalmed. And preliminary findings on the three in the beds at the April house are the same. They were embalmed a long time ago."

"Seriously?" Sarge said.

Robin nodded. "That's what he said."

"Well, that explains why no neighbors caught any smell," Pickett said.

"There would still be some," Robin said, "but if the bodies were left out to dry in the hot air and good ventilation, they would mummify very quickly in this dry air after being embalmed."

"Lott and Julia and Ander dealt with a millionaire serial killer," Sarge said, "who was embalming bodies and dumping them in a lake up in Idaho."

"They did?" Robin asked.

"I remember hearing about it," Pickett said, nodding. Lott and Julia and Ander were the three retired detectives who started the Cold Poker Gang task force. "Right before we joined the Gang."

"Happened while I was away from the Gang for a short time," Sarge said. "The killer was just using the embalming and a chain of mortuaries to kill his victims and make them disappear after he got done with them. Very different than leaving them in a bed or buried in a basement."

They sat in silence for a few moments letting the sounds of the morning buffet wash over them. Pickett was pretty sure she didn't want to know anything more about that case, especially after dealing right now with this one.

"Any idea how the girls all died in that first house?" Sarge asked after a moment.

"Blunt force trauma on the one, the first one they dug up," Robin said. "Nothing else, but the medical folks are just getting started and that will take a few days, including DNA, even rushed."

Pickett just sat there staring at the remains of the omelet on her plate, then pushed it away. She was no longer hungry at all.

"I'll get digging on those houses and the money trails from Benjamin States," Robin said. "See if I can connect him to those houses today. And see if I can connect an embalmer anywhere along the history of this mess."

"Those houses really are memorial tombs," Sarge said.

Pickett only nodded to that. And there were still four more they hadn't looked into yet.

And she wasn't going to.

Those could be left to the active detectives. She already had enough nightmares after two.

More than enough.

And they still had the first one to finish searching today.

CHAPTER THIRTEEN

June 12th, 2017
Las Vegas, Nevada

Sarge stared at the March house as Pickett drove up and parked. It now had crime scene tape around it and a guard sitting in a marked car out front. The poor guy had clearly been there all night.

Sarge remembered that kind of duty when he was first getting started on the force. Guarding a crime scene all night. Nothing got more boring.

Nothing.

At that moment Cavanaugh pulled up and again parked in the driveway behind the old car in the carport. Sarge wondered if anyone had searched that car yet. He doubted it. That was what they were here for today.

Cavanaugh, a massive cup of coffee in one hand, climbed out of the car, waved at them, and went to the patrol car to send the poor cop on his way home.

Pickett shut off her car and they climbed out, carrying bottles of water from the cooler they had strapped by a seatbelt on the back seat.

The sun was just breaking over the hills, giving the air a fresh, bright look to it. The temperature was still comfortable with a slight breeze, so with luck they could open up the house and get some air flowing through it before it got too hot.

"Just got active detectives headed to the other four house addresses I got from Robin," Cavanaugh said.

"I don't think I could take searching another one of these horror places," Pickett said.

"I'm feeling the exact same way," Cavanaugh said.

They went to the front door and Cavanaugh moved the tape and they opened the place up.

It smelled of dry dust and age and was far warmer than it was outside.

"Lab folks have been all over the place already," Cavanaugh said, "but let's still wear gloves in case they want to come back. But first we open up the doors and windows."

It took them just a moment to get all the blinds lifted and windows open throughout the place. A bunch of the pictures of naked girls had been taken by the lab techs, but not all of them by a long ways.

"Looks like there are five different girls' pictures on these walls," Cavanaugh said. "The ones in the bedroom on the right seem to be of a girl that isn't here."

Sarge glanced at Pickett and she nodded.

"Let's go out front where it's cooler to talk," Sarge said. "Give this place a chance to cool down."

Cavanaugh in his oversized jacket led the way, going to his car and taking it off and tossing it across the front seat. He had on suspenders holding up his pants and a shoulder holster for his gun and his badge on his belt.

Sarge took off his light jacket that hid his gun and badge as well and Pickett did the same with her jacket, taking them both to her car and coming back with their bottles of water.

Cavanaugh was still working on his coffee.

"Robin has done her magic again," Pickett said. "She managed to find the real name of this Ben person."

Cavanaugh looked surprised.

They told him how she had done it with facial recognition and high school yearbooks and who his name was.

"And he's still alive," Sarge said, "and supposedly married to Cathy Wendt, the girl that started all this."

Cavanaugh damned near dropped his coffee, which would have been a critical emergency for any detective this early in the morning.

"They are both still alive," Pickett said, "living in a big estate out north of town. Robin doesn't think he knows anything about all of this, even though she has traced the money and buying these homes to him."

Cavanaugh just shook his head. "We got no proof on anyone on this. Except circumstantial with that dead guy in the basement. And we have no idea who he is."

"Think we need some officers sitting on the guy?" Sarge asked.

"Can Robin do that electronically for now?" Cavanaugh asked.

"Let me find out," Pickett said.

She quickly called Robin and asked.

Then Pickett laughed and hung up, smiling. "She's already doing that. She will know when they sleep, flush the toilet, and what they are eating. They won't move without her tracing them. But officially she is not doing that, of course."

"Of course," Cavanaugh said, laughing. "Tell her unofficially thanks. Saved a couple cops some nasty duty for a while."

"I will," Pickett said.

"Embalmed, huh?" Sarge said.

Cavanaugh nodded and finished off his coffee, putting the cup on the roof of his car. "So, ready to see if we can find anything that will help us in that horror house?"

"No," Pickett said.

"We'll just stand out here and cheer you on," Sarge said.

Cavanaugh looked at both of them. "Not damned funny."

"Yes it was," Pickett said, smiling and turning Cavanaugh toward the house and walking with him.

"It was," Sarge said, laughing as he followed them back into a place he really had no desire to ever go again.

CHAPTER FOURTEEN

June 12th, 2017
Las Vegas, Nevada

Two hours later the air was starting to heat up and Pickett was covered in dust and sweat. They had carefully looked at every surface through the entire place and found nothing, not even a stray old receipt.

They had moved out into the carport and checked out the car. Pickett stood back and to one side as Cavanaugh popped the trunk. It would not have surprised her that a body was in there, but thankfully just a spare and a jack and nothing under any of it.

There wasn't even anything in the glove box or down under the seats. The car was dirty, but not one detail of who actually had operated it. The owner of record on the books was Ben March. But they had been hoping for more.

As they were standing in the carport, Pickett noticed a wooden ladder leaning against the side of the house under the carport. And that reminded her of one thing they had all forgotten.

"Don't these old homes have small attics?"

Sarge looked at her and Cavanaugh just shook his head.

"I seem to remember an opening in the ceiling of the closet on the left side of the hallway," she said. She had noticed it in the search, but hadn't thought anything about it.

Sarge walked out onto the driveway and studied the roofline. Then he came back nodding. "A person couldn't stand up, but a lot of room up there."

"Ladder is what made me think of it," Pickett said, pointing to the ladder sitting against the wall.

"Last place we check," Sarge said, going over and grabbing the eight-foot tall ladder.

He looked at Cavanaugh. "I'll carry, you climb."

"Just because I am younger than you, right?" Cavanaugh asked as they went back inside and to the bedroom.

"Yeah," Sarge said. "That's it."

When they got to the closet, Pickett pointed out the ladder marks on the wall up high.

"Didn't even notice those," Cavanaugh said, shaking his head. "Maybe I really do need to retire."

"Eighteen more days," Pickett said.

"Who's counting?" Cavanaugh said.

Sarge got the ladder in place and Cavanaugh went up a couple steps, making sure each step was solid, then he pushed open the piece of wood blocking the hole, shoving it to one side.

Sarge handed him a flashlight and Cavanaugh went up two more steps and shined his light around.

Then he said softly, "This can't be happening."

He came down and handed Sarge the flashlight and indicated he should look. "I got some phone calls to make."

He headed out of the bedroom.

Pickett watched him go, then looked back at Sarge. "Do we really want to see what is up there?"

"No," Sarge said. "But after that reaction, I can't not look."

She agreed. She couldn't not look either.

Sarge climbed the ladder in the closet while Pickett held it steady.

Pickett watched from below as Sarge shined the powerful flashlight around.

All Pickett could see was him shaking his head.

Then he came down and handed the flashlight to her. "Not pretty and not something you are going to see every day."

She took the light and went up the ladder, convinced she shouldn't.

She had to go another two steps higher than Sarge or Cavanaugh before she got into the attic enough to see.

It felt hot already up here. She could only imagine how hot it got during the summer days.

There were pieces of plywood covering over the ceiling joists so a person could walk down the middle bent over. She was short enough, she might be able to stand almost upright without banging her head on a roof joist.

But not a chance in hell was she climbing up in there.

She could see the length of the house and on both sides of the middle walkway were bodies stacked on top of one another. All fully dressed, all mummified.

More accurately, baked to a strange, sickly brown color.

And all different ages and races, from what she could tell. Young, old, men, women. All were dressed, at least from the waist up, in dress clothes. At one point they had been in caskets, from the looks of them.

They were stacked like cordwood along both sides. Some face up, some face down into the person below them.

She was numb.

There had to be a hundred bodies up here. And from the looks of it, they had all been here a very, very long time, baking in the summer heat. More than likely for decades.

She had been calling this a house of horrors before now.

The place had now officially earned its name twice over.

She climbed down slowly, handed Sarge the light, and asked, "Can we now get out of this place and never come back?"

"Please," Sarge said.

She led the way down the hall and out the front door.

Cavanaugh was standing beside his car, talking on the phone. She could only imagine the ground-shaking movement this discovery was making in the chief's office.

And there were five more houses that could possibly be just like this one.

This one was bad enough.

And she had a hunch that right now, as of this discovery, the Cold Poker Gang task force was officially off this case. They only dealt with cold cases.

Finding a hundred-plus bodies in one house was now far from cold, even though every person in the house had been dead and roasting in that attic a very long time.

PART THREE

Not Dead Yet

CHAPTER FIFTEEN

June 15th, 2017
Las Vegas, Nevada

For the last three days, Sarge had been very relieved that he and Pickett had been off this case and away from those horror houses.

Robin had stayed in contact with Cavanaugh and had kept digging. So this morning at breakfast, she was going to fill them in on what the police had found so far.

And what she had found as well.

The morning air still had a little bite to it, but Sarge had no doubt today was going to be a pretty standard warm June day. Might not hit a hundred, but during the peak time in the afternoon, it might get close.

But now the air was comfortable. The tourists were calm and not many around, so the walk from their condo to the Golden Nugget was easy and enjoyable.

And both of them were curious as to what was going on.

Somehow, the entire thing hadn't hit the news yet, which stunned Sarge and Pickett. This should have been a front page, top-of-the-paper story and lead news on every television station. In fact, this should have been on all the national newscasts as well.

Somehow, it wasn't even mentioned and Sarge really wanted to know why. He couldn't believe the department had kept it quiet. No chance of that. Not something this big and with so many people having to be involved with it.

No, the paper and radio stations and television stations were holding this story for some reason and Sarge hoped Robin would know why. And it had to be something larger than hurting tourism, although that reason had gotten a lot of stories downplayed or killed over the years.

They got to the buffet ahead of Robin and since it was his turn to buy, he paid for all three of them while Pickett went ahead to the food. The place smelled so wonderful and rich, with bacon and waffle smells filling the air, he almost didn't want to stop to pay.

He hadn't realized how hungry he really was this morning.

He wasn't far behind her, since the tourist rush was over and there were only about forty people in the large place, most over at tables against the pool windows. No one was sitting near their favorite table.

He had just gotten his omelet and waffle when Robin appeared at the top of the escalator coming up from the casino to the buffet. He waved her in, signaling she was already paid, and took his food back over to the table.

He and Pickett were half done eating by the time Robin joined them.

For the first ten minutes, as Robin dug into her food, they talked about the three cats and how calm and peaceful the last three days had been for them. They had seen five movies in total, three at night at home and two they had actually gone out to a theater.

"So," Sarge said, stacking his empty plates to one side, "I am dying to know why the media is sitting on this one."

"Families," Robin said. "All those bodies in the attics were supposed to have been cremated thirty and forty years ago."

"Oh, shit," Pickett said.

"Attics?" Sarge asked.

Robin nodded. "All six houses were almost identical. Young blonde girls in beds and buried in the basements, naked pictures on the walls, and bodies stacked in the attics."

Sarge sat back in his chair. He couldn't even think of anything to ask. That was just too much to try to grasp.

"Stunning, isn't it?" Robin said. "I've been trying to get a handle on this for days. Forget all the young girls' bodies in the beds for the moment. The police have to identify and contact well over five hundred families that their grandmother or grandfather or mother or father wasn't really cremated and the ashes they got back were fake. And all from deaths forty years ago."

Sarge just shook his head. "Impossible."

"Matching a body with the right date-of-death is a nightmare all by itself," Robin said. "The media is holding off until they clear out every relative they can find easily, then the media will run with it to try to get the relatives that can't be found and that still care to come out of the woodwork."

"Do they know who did this?"

"No," Robin said. "They know the bodies were supposedly shipped to the county's only crematorium out on the old Boulder Highway from a dozen different mortuaries around town. Back in the early 1970s, pretty much every person who was to be cremated in Las Vegas during those years ended up in the attics of these six houses. Cremation back then was not accepted as much as it is now, so very few opted for it."

"And even though it was only one place, there is still no idea who did this?" Sarge asked. He couldn't believe that was possible.

"Nope," Robin said. "The crematorium was torn down in nineteen-eighty-one so a subdivision could be built, which was pretty much when the last body was put in the attics. That part of the industry was hardly regulated back then in Nevada anyway. And the owner of the crematorium used a fake name."

"Of course," Pickett said.

"They must have made a fortune taking payments for bodies and doing nothing," Sarge said.

He knew that for the longest time, the funeral business was full of scams and fakes. Thankfully, over the last thirty years, new restrictions and rules and organizations had stepped in to keep that sort of thing down to a minimum.

And even though there were five hundred bodies in those attics, the only crime would be fraud and mistreatment of a corpse, both long past statutes of limitations.

This was just a massive PR nightmare.

And all of this had happened before those sorts of government regulations and licensing on the funeral industry came into play. In fact, the years this was happening, the mob and Howard Hughes had just cleared the city and everything was trying to find a new balance.

Sarge just shook his head. "So we have six houses full of bodies. Each house is owned by someone with the fake names of a kid who went to high school as a junior eight years in a row? Right?"

Robin nodded.

"And what about Benjamin Ronald States?" Pickett asked.

"No connection that we can find in the slightest," Robin said. "No one has even gone to talk with him about any of this yet because there is no connection."

"Police a little busy, huh?" Sarge asked, shaking his head.

"Is Cavanaugh going to survive this?" Pickett asked.

"I've talked with him twice a day and he seems to be his normal grumpy self," Robin said. "And the chief has pulled him off of the mortuary problem and has him focused back on the young blondes. They are not mortuary victims, even though they were also embalmed. They are murders."

"How many young girls did it end up being?" Sarge asked, afraid of the answer.

"Thirty-one," Robin said.

"Wow," Pickett said.

"The chief wants us back helping Cavanaugh," Robin said.

Sarge nodded. Part of him was glad to be able to be back on this case. But another part had really liked not thinking about this horror show.

"As long as we don't have to go anywhere near any of those houses," Pickett said.

"I doubt we will," Robin said. "Those are locked down solid and the city is hauling out bodies at night from each home to a few mortuaries who are helping out. They don't want the word out on this either because of the damage it would do to their industry."

"Makes sense," Sarge said. "So any updates on any of the tests on the girls?"

"And the guy in the basement of that first house?" Pickett asked.

Sarge kept forgetting about that guy.

Robin frowned and nodded. "The girls were all killed with

blunt force trauma to the back of the head. All with a similar or same weapon."

"So we had a serial killer," Pickett said.

Sarge agreed, especially with the past tense on this. Looked like the killer operated for a short few years and then stopped for some reason.

Or at least Sarge hoped he or she stopped and didn't just move out of town and start up again.

He didn't even want to think of that possibility.

CHAPTER SIXTEEN

June 15th, 2017
Las Vegas, Nevada

All three of them had out their notebooks and were trying to figure out what to do next. They had all gotten some more fruit and Sarge had gotten some bacon and they had settled in to work.

All three of them were drinking coffee. Pickett figured it was going to be one of those kind of days when coffee was a very good idea. She hadn't expected the chief to let them back on these cases just yet, but she was glad he had. The regular detectives were just too busy with the mess from all those attics.

"So we forget about the attic stuff," Sarge said. "Let's go over exactly what we do have."

Pickett and Robin both nodded. Pickett figured that if they didn't concentrate down, they would never have even a slight chance of solving this one.

"First," Sarge said, "we have a guy named Ben who came

into town, registered as a junior in high school under a fake name, and then did it again for eight straight years, moving from school to school and name to name. Right?"

Robin nodded.

Pickett wrote that down, then put a big "Why" beside the question.

"On another topic, but somehow maybe related," Sarge said, "we have a girl by the name of Cathy Wendt who went missing in June of 1977. She was a junior and her boyfriend's name was Ben. Right?"

"And you traced that Ben from pictures of him in Cathy Wendt's missing person's files to a Benjamin Ronald States, who is still alive and married to Cathy Wendt," Pickett said to Robin.

"Yes," Robin said. "The connection becomes broken when we looked up the old records for a Ben March and he supposedly lived at the house where we found the first bodies. We first thought that Ben March was the same Ben, now we do not know for sure."

"So we have no idea if Ben March is Benjamin States?" Sarge asked a moment before Pickett could.

"That is correct," Robin said. "I have no connection in money or anything else from States to the fake name of March and that house. Or any of the houses."

"Any idea who the guy was in the basement?" Sarge asked.

Robin shook her head. "We should be getting the first rushed DNA tests back on him and those first girls today or tomorrow. Kind of doubt that will help us much unless we get lucky somehow."

Robin looked at some notes, then said, "We do know the old guy in the chair died of dehydration and natural causes. They put his age in the mid-seventies."

Pickett was stunned. "That old? That meant he had to be in

his mid-thirties, if not slightly older when those girls were killed."

"Would look that way," Robin said.

Pickett wrote that in her notebook. She had a gut sense that had something to do with all of this, but not a clue what that might be.

All the victims of the murders were about the same age, as best as could be figured without a lot of work. All wore their hair blonde, all were killed in the same fashion, and all were embalmed.

"So on the victims," Pickett said, "our killer had access to a way to embalm his victims."

"Twenty-one official mortuaries in Las Vegas in that time period," Robin said. "Those were the official ones. Embalming was something that could be done by most anyone with the skill and supplies and some basic equipment."

Pickett marked that down and wrote "Dead End" beside it.

"The pictures are another crazy part of this," Sarge said. "How did someone, and for what reason, get those girls to naturally undress for nude pictures?"

"Maybe the promise of being in a major magazine like *Playboy* or *Penthouse* or one of the others men's magazines at the time," Robin said.

Pickett nodded. "That might do it. A promise of money and fame."

"And back then Polaroid pictures were a standard way of doing test shots for major photo shoots," Sarge said, "since the things developed in a minute or so."

"And taking that many of them would be a normal thing for a professional photographer to do," Pickett said. "Could those houses have been used as a form of photography business at one point?"

"I'll look though old newspaper ads and such and see what I can find," Robin said, nodding.

Pickett marked down in her book "Pictures." Then she put a "Possible" beside it.

And that was where they stopped. They seemed to have a lot of information, but all natural ways of looking into all this was blocked by a solid barrier of forty years of time.

So much had changed since the early seventies. Pickett felt like they were living in a different world, the more they looked back through those forty years.

Then it dawned on her that maybe they weren't looking exactly right. They were focused on the eight years and six houses.

She looked up at Sarge, then at Robin. "What happened during the thirty-plus years since all this went on and when that guy died in that basement and the power got turned off to all those houses?"

Sarge just blinked at her.

Robin swore softly and wrote in her notebook.

They needed to start last year, with modern techniques, and trace backwards. And Pickett knew exactly where to start.

"The cars," Pickett said. "We start with the cars and work backwards. There have to be cameras and other records in car lots and at the Department of Motor Vehicles."

Both Sarge and Robin nodded and both kept writing in their notebooks, which was a very good sign.

CHAPTER SEVENTEEN

June 15th, 2017
Las Vegas, Nevada

Sarge really liked the idea that they start with the cars. Turns out each house had a car parked in the driveway. And all were as clean as the one they had first looked at. It made no sense, but Pickett was right, it was a way to bring this investigation to now and work backwards.

And there was another way, but Sarge figured it was a long shot.

"How about we go talk with Benjamin States," he said.

"Think Cavanaugh could get that approved at this point?"

Robin shrugged. "Let me find out."

She took her phone out of her bag and hit a number and put the phone to her ear. "Cavanaugh," she said. "Got the gang here finishing breakfast and getting ready to go to work."

She listened for a moment, then nodded. "We're wondering

if you could arrange for us, with you along if you have time, to go talk with Benjamin States and his wife."

She listened, then laughed. "Fire me the address. Sarge and Pickett will meet you there. I've got some tracing to do on those six cars we found."

She listened for a moment, then said "Thanks," and hung up.

"He already got it approved and figured we would ask, so he called the couple and set up an appointment in one hour at their home."

Pickett laughed and Sarge just shook his head.

"Cavanaugh is going to be a great addition to this task force," Sarge said.

"If the paperwork on this case doesn't kill him first," Pickett said, and they all laughed.

Fifty-five minutes later, after a brisk walk back to the condo to get the car and some ice in an ice chest and bottles of water, they made it to Benjamin States' gated home on a sprawling acreage overlooking the Las Vegas valley.

"Wow," Pickett said as they drove slowly up the twisting drive through the rocks and desert plants toward the big white stucco mansion that seemed to spread over the top of the rock bluff.

Sarge could only agree. It was an impressive place.

And expensive. Millions and millions expensive.

They pulled up and stopped in front of the home on a massive circular driveway. Pickett left the car running to keep the air-conditioning going and they both got a bottle of water from the cooler.

They didn't dare make a move until Cavanaugh was with them. This was still an active case after all and they needed an active detective.

It seemed very strange to be working a live case again. Very strange.

A few moments later Cavanaugh pulled in behind them.

He met them beside Pickett's Jeep and indicated the house. "You two are rich, why don't you live in a place like this?"

"We're not that rich," Pickett said.

"And we can't walk to breakfast either," Sarge said, pointing back toward the city in the distance. This place was beautiful, but it was a way out of town.

"Yeah, good point there," Cavanaugh said. "I'll let you off the hook this time."

"Thanks," Pickett said, laughing. "You getting any sleep?"

"Like a log for four hours a night. Two naps a day when I can catch them. I plan on getting old enough to join you guys in the Gang."

"Fifteen days," Pickett said.

"Oh, really, I had lost track," Cavanaugh said, then laughed.

The three of them turned to the massive ornate wood front door of the big mansion. The door was so huge, it either had to be balanced perfectly or it would need a machine to open it. Sarge figured it to be almost two stories tall.

Turned out, after they knocked, it opened easily in perfect balance to show an even larger and more ornate stone and tile and rough wood room beyond.

The man that met them was medium height, wearing tan slacks, a light shirt, and slippers. He had his gray hair cut short and had striking blue eyes. He looked to be in his fifties or early sixties and was clearly in great shape.

He introduced himself as Benjamin States, but that they could call him Ben. They shook his hand and gave their names and showed their badges. He then asked them to come in.

He led them through the massive tile-floored and high-ceilinged front foyer with a staircase that looked like it might go on forever upward. They ended the trip in what looked to be a library, with maple shelving and walls full of expensive leather books.

The place had a wonderful warm feel, which surprised Sarge considering the rest of the house had felt cold. And the room smelled a little of the remains of breakfast, so the kitchen must be close by as well.

There was a rock fireplace filling one wall with a large television hung over the mantel and two comfortable recliners facing it.

Two couches framed the seating area with a large wooden coffee table in the center, covered mostly in magazines.

At that moment an older woman with short gray hair and a bright smile came into the room. She seemed to also be in great shape.

Her husband did the introductions, introducing her as his wife, Cathy.

They all took a seat, Sarge and Pickett on one couch, Cavanaugh on the other, and the two States in their respective reading chairs.

"So, detectives, what can we do to help you?" Ben asked.

"Well," Cavanaugh said, sitting forward. "We have a real mess on our hands and we don't even know where to start. So let me have Pickett and Sarge here tell you how they got all this started and how your names got into the investigation."

Both Cathy and Ben frowned, but nodded.

"Pickett and I are members of a cold case special task force," Sarge said. "We were handed the very cold case of a missing girl by the name of Cathy Wendt."

Sarge was watching Cathy's reaction and she instantly had one, sitting back and then looking at Ben.

"We had very little to go on," Pickett said, "considering that was forty years ago. So we talked to the brother who was of no help, then we went to Cathy Wendt's old boyfriend's home."

Sarge watched as Ben nodded on that.

"The power had been turned off for about a year and inside we found a number of things," Sarge said. "First, we found a man sitting in a rocking chair in the basement, staring at the graves of three young girls. He had dug up one of them a little."

"Oh, my," Cathy said, covering her mouth.

"We thought at first that one of them was Cathy Wendt and her boyfriend, Ben March, had killed her," Pickett said. "But it turns out there was another mummified body of a young girl with blonde hair in a bed upstairs. All of the four of them had been dead for a very long time, more than likely since the seventies. We have yet to identify any of them."

Sarge was watching Ben and Cathy and they seemed seriously stunned and shocked. A normal reaction to hearing something like that.

"Here is where things get even stranger," Sarge said, skipping the part about bodies in the attic for now. "There was a picture of Cathy and Ben in the missing person's file. We ran a facial recognition scan on Ben's face and found that he was really Benjamin Ronald States, twenty-three at the time, who moved to Las Vegas in 1975."

"And we know that you are Cathy Wendt, our missing person from 1977," Pickett said to Cathy.

Cathy nodded and looked to her husband, who only nodded.

"Ben got me away from my father and mother," Cathy said. "I was sixteen and of age for the time in Las Vegas, so we did nothing illegal. But I knew that if I didn't vanish, my parents would not let me leave. In fact, I was certain they would kill me if I tried. To say the least, I came from a very abusive family."

"So we left town for six months," Ben said, "living in Washington state and in Canada for most of it. Then we came back."

"I dyed my hair brown," Cathy said, "always wore sunglasses when I went out for years, and we managed to avoid my parents and brother and friends. No one knew until now."

"So you were Ben March?" Sarge asked.

Ben nodded. "I assume you know if you traced when I got out here that I changed my name and enrolled as a junior every year for eight years in different schools. I met Cathy on the third year of doing that and we have been together ever since."

"And you had that three-bedroom house under your Ben March name?"

"I did," Ben said, nodding. "When we left town I put it on the market and it sold within a month or so. I have no idea what happened to it. I never checked."

Cavanaugh looked at his notebook and then asked Ben about the other five homes.

Ben nodded with each. "I owned them all for one year each, paid cash for them, sold them at a slight profit after a year."

"We would fix them up some," Cathy said. "New paint, new carpet, make a little profit. It was fun for me to help with as I was going to college."

"The records we could find show that you still own all those homes," Sarge said. "Under your different names."

"Not a chance," Ben said, now clearly upset. "I was paid for those homes by my broker. Never had another thing to do with them."

"We know that," Pickett said.

Cavanaugh nodded and Ben seemed to relax some.

"We know that somehow the records were falsified," Sarge

said, "to leave your fake name on the home, but we can't figure out why just yet."

"So if you don't mind my asking," Pickett said, "why did you buy those homes and sign up as a junior in different schools every year?"

"To meet girls," Ben said, then he smiled at Cathy.

Cathy nodded. "He's telling you the truth. Ben is a world-famous photographer of nudes. His work hangs all over the world in galleries."

"We know that as well," Cavanaugh said, nodding.

"So with him as a junior and me as his girlfriend from another school, he could meet girls who wanted to do some modeling. We used the homes to not only fix up to sell, but for a studio."

"Magazine work?" Pickett asked.

"Some at first," Ben said. "But the magazines of that time were turning more toward porn than erotica and I stopped. It was in about that time period that we started our company and the photography went from the main focus to a background work."

"Now it is back as the main focus," Cathy said.

Sarge looked at her. She was clearly very proud of her husband's work.

"Did you take Polaroid pictures of the models to start with?" Pickett asked.

"I did," Ben said.

"What happened to all those pictures?" Sarge asked.

"They were destroyed in 1981 when the building that I leased a small office and darkroom from burnt down."

"Luckily we had most of the negatives of his important photos and all the records at home," Cathy said.

Sarge just nodded. Now they at least understood a little

more of what had happened. Clearly these two had had a stalker back then who not only followed them, but killed some of his models, stole those pictures, and burnt down his darkroom.

"Did the model releases survive the fire?" Pickett asked.

"They did," Ben said. "They were also at home."

Sarge looked at Picket and then at Cavanaugh. It seemed that maybe, just maybe, they had caught a break.

CHAPTER EIGHTEEN

June 15th, 2017
Las Vegas, Nevada

Ben and Cathy asked the three of them to join them in the kitchen.

"Sorry for my manners," Cathy said. "I should have offered you all a drink."

"Oh, we're fine, ma'am," Cavanaugh said, smiling his best and most friendly smile.

The kitchen was state of the art, as Pickett would have expected, but also very comfortable. Rough, natural-colored wooden beams ran across the ceiling and old-style pendant lights hung down over a massive island covered in quartz.

Three skylights in the high ceiling also let in natural light.

The place had a wonderful faint odor of bacon, more than likely cooked for breakfast.

Cathy got all three of the detectives a glass of ice water, Ben a glass of iced tea, and herself a glass of some sort of juice with ice.

"So I am assuming that since you mentioned my model releases, you would like to see them?" Ben asked.

"If we could," Cavanaugh said. "We will, of course, keep all information in them completely private."

"Why?" Ben asked. "I have a feeling there is something you are not telling us."

"We believe the girls found dead in that house might have been your models," Pickett said.

Both Ben and Cathy looked puzzled. Both shook their heads.

Pickett was absolutely sure that they had nothing to do with this. They didn't seem to be covering anything up. But there was just no telling.

Sarge looked at Cavanaugh and he nodded, so Sarge turned to Ben. "The Polaroid pictures you took were on the walls of the houses. Thousands of them total in each house."

Cathy and Ben looked like they were going to be sick.

"How is that possible?" Cathy asked.

"We'll investigate the fire to your darkroom and office building," Pickett said. "But just guessing, someone broke in there, stole them all, and set the place on fire."

"Would they have also gotten the names of the models from records there?" Sarge asked.

Ben nodded slowly.

"I think I'm going to be sick," Cathy said.

Ben reached over and touched her hand, which seemed to calm her some. Clearly these two had been in love for a very long time. And were still good for each other.

"How many girls?" Ben asked after a long moment of silence in the big kitchen.

Pickett glanced at Cavanaugh, who shook his head slightly. Clearly he wanted to keep the number secret.

"We honestly don't know yet," Pickett said, "because there is another factor clogging up the investigation and making it much worse."

"Worse than this?" Cathy asked, her voice a little shrill.

"We need you to promise for a time to keep what we are about to tell you to yourselves completely," Cavanaugh said.

Both nodded.

"Each house had a small attic," Sarge said.

Both Ben and Cathy nodded.

"The attics were full of bodies that should have been cremated, but were not."

"Full?" Ben asked.

Sarge nodded.

"Right now the police and the press are keeping a lid on this until families can be notified. But it seems for about six years or so, all the bodies in the entire Las Vegas area that were to be cremated instead ended up stored in the attics of those homes."

"Oh, god, no," Cathy said, covering her mouth and turning and running from the room.

Ben watched her go. He had his back to the detectives.

Then he seemed to gather himself together and turned back to them. "Were all the victims blonde? Like Cathy used to be?"

"Yes," Cavanaugh said. "And Polaroid pictures of Cathy were on one wall. In a room without a body."

"Were all the bodies embalmed?" Ben asked.

Now it was Sarge and Pickett and Cavanaugh's turn to be shocked.

Pickett was surprised that either this guy was admitting he did it, or if he had, he was really stunningly good at acting.

"Yes, they were," Cavanaugh said. "But no one knows that either. How did you guess that?"

"The monster that was Cathy's father embalmed bodies for a living," Ben said. "The son-of-a-bitch clearly must have always known where we were."

Pickett just stared at Sarge.

And silence hung over the room until Cavanaugh took out his phone and called the lab.

"DNA results in on the old man in the basement?"

Pickett watched as Cavanaugh listened.

"Compare the old man against the DNA sample from Cathy Wendt's brother. Get back to me as quickly as you can."

He hung up.

Ben was nodding and looking troubled.

Then Ben said, "Excuse me, I need to go see how Cathy is doing. We will be right back."

As Ben left, Pickett took out her phone and called Robin. They had their first real lead on all of this, and if it panned out, might answer a ton of questions.

If it panned out.

And honestly, Pickett felt like it just might.

And that worried her.

CHAPTER NINETEEN

June 15th, 2017
Las Vegas, Nevada

Sarge watched as Ben brought Cathy back into the warm and comfortable kitchen and had her sit at the counter and sip on her juice.

"I'm sorry for my reaction," Cathy said after a moment.

"Completely understandable," Pickett said. "We came in here and blindsided you with all this stuff from the ancient past."

Cathy nodded. "I was in counseling for over ten years because of what that monster of a father did to me. Ben rescued me from my father and mother."

Sarge watched, as did Cavanaugh and Pickett. Sarge had a hunch that if anyone could talk to Cathy, it would be Pickett.

"So your father was an undertaker?" Pickett asked.

"No," Cathy said. "Just an embalmer. But he loved dead

bodies. He used to make Mom and I lay naked on the kitchen table and pretend we were dead."

"Your mother helped with his sickness?" Pickett asked.

Sarge could tell that Pickett was now really shocked, even though he knew she shouldn't be. Mothers often helped facilitate child abuse by simply pretending it never happened. Pickett knew that.

Sometimes it was because the wives feared the husband, sometimes because back fifty years or more ago, the women looked away because they didn't think it was wrong. Fathers owned the wife and the children and could do what they wanted with them.

Things had really changed for the better in that area.

Cathy nodded. "My mother was a beaten, controlled, mind-dead woman by the time I left. She helped the monster and never protected me. Then refused to talk with me about it, as if it never happened. I actually think she enjoyed it, to be honest."

Sarge felt like he wanted to be sick now. No matter how long on the force you dealt with the sick and perverted of humanity, a person never got used to it. Especially when it came to what adults did to children.

Cavanaugh was just staring down at the pattern in the quartz countertop, not moving.

"So you think your father might have discovered what you and Ben were doing after you vanished?" Pickett asked.

"We saw no evidence of that until you brought this here now," Ben said. "But embalming the girls and the bodies in the attic make sense for it to be him. He was that sick. And I am sure he wanted to get back at me for taking Cathy from him."

Sarge nodded. It did make sense. That would explain leaving Ben's fake name on the houses.

"Why didn't he just report you?" Pickett asked.

"Because he knew that if he did I would tell the world what he was doing to me and my mother," Cathy said, coldness in her voice. "And I would have, too."

Ben nodded to that. "We considered turning him in a number of times. But it was the 1970s and times were very different then. Things were only starting to change, but parents still had the say over the kids and could do what they wanted with them. Everyone, including the police, just looked the other way."

Sarge remembered that well from his early days on the force.

"Any idea how he might have gotten to all those bodies stashed in the attic?" Cavanaugh asked.

Both Cathy and Ben shook their heads.

"We paid no attention to him as we tried to build our lives," Ben said.

At that point Cavanaugh's phone buzzed and he looked at it and then said, "Excuse me for a moment."

He clicked on the phone and said, "Yeah."

He listened, then said, "Thank you."

He hung up and looked directly at Cathy and Ben. "You no longer ever have to worry about that man. It was his body we found in the basement of the March house. They matched his DNA to your brother."

Cathy just shook her head.

Ben looked sick.

"That's not good news?" Pickett asked.

Cathy shook her head and clearly couldn't speak.

Finally Ben said, "Her brother had a different father."

"Oh," Pickett said. "Do you know that man's name?"

Cathy and Ben both shook their heads no.

"My mom told me once, in private, that I should never tell my father. She said she had gotten tired of my father's perverted games and wanted real sex, so she met a guy and got pregnant. She never told me who that was."

"Oh," Pickett said again.

All Sarge could do was the same thing Cavanaugh was doing, stare at the pattern in the quartz countertop in front of him.

CHAPTER TWENTY

June 15th, 2017
Las Vegas, Nevada

Pickett didn't know what to think at this point.

Cathy, looking very pale, finally asked to be excused to go lie down.

Ben walked her out of the room after telling Cavanaugh he would be back with the model records and releases after he got Cathy resting.

Pickett glanced at Sarge, then at Cavanaugh, when it was only the three of them in the kitchen. "I think they are telling the truth," she said, her voice low.

Cavanaugh nodded.

So did Sarge.

"So Cathy's brother's father is the dead guy in the basement," Sarge said. "But we still don't know who he was."

"Maybe the brother will tell us if he knows," Cavanaugh said.

"Cathy knew her father had a sexual thing for dead women," Pickett said. "Any chance there is any way of knowing if those women were sexually abused after they were killed?"

Cavanaugh shrugged at that. "Mummy sex? I suppose in Las Vegas anything is possible."

Pickett tried not to laugh as Cavanaugh took out his phone and called a number with one button. After a moment he said, "Cavanaugh again. Got another question for you on the blonde girl victims from the houses. Any chance you can tell if their bodies were sexually abused."

He listened for a minute, then his eyes got wide and he just sat there, listening and shaking his head.

Pickett was completely sure that if the news got to Cavanaugh like that, she wasn't going to want to hear it.

Finally Cavanaugh said, "Could you send that report to Robin on the Cold Case Task Force, please."

He nodded, then said, "Thank you."

He clicked off his phone and glanced around to make sure that Ben wasn't coming back into the room.

Then he leaned forward and said softly, "The four girls in the first house were all embalmed. All had their private parts sewn open so that they would be easy to have sex with after they were dead."

"Now I want to be sick," Pickett said.

Sarge just shook his head. This case was going beyond disgusting and right down into totally unthinkable.

"It gets worse," Cavanaugh said.

"How can that get worse?" Sarge asked.

Pickett wanted to ask the same question. How could it be worse than that?

Cavanaugh looked around to make sure Ben hadn't returned then he said simply, "The girl's body under the sheet was dressed in a sheer nightgown and there are signs of at least five or six different DNA semen samples in the body in the bed, plus lubricant. Some of it seemingly fresh. They are working to try to get DNA."

Sarge glanced at Pickett who was as pale as Cathy had looked a moment ago.

He took a deep breath and took a large drink of the water in front of him.

Pickett did the same.

"And it goes on," Cavanaugh said, after also taking a drink.

"I am pretty sure I don't want to know what 'goes on' means," Pickett said.

Sarge nodded.

Cavanaugh looked around again, then once again leaned forward. "The body half dug-up in the basement with the hair and the hand showing?"

"Don't tell me," Sarge sat back.

Pickett wanted to just cover her ears.

Cavanaugh nodded. "Semen all over the hand and in the hair from numbers of men."

There was not a thing any of them could say to that.

Three hardened, Las Vegas career detectives, shocked to their cores.

CHAPTER TWENTY-ONE

June 15th, 2017
Las Vegas, Nevada

Pickett was sipping on the ice water, trying to clear her mind, when Ben returned carrying an old file box that looked dusty and had clearly seen the wear of years.

"Sorry about the dust on this stuff," he said. "Been saving it to donate to some university collection somewhere, after I die. Cathy's idea."

He set the box on the counter and opened the lid, showing neat rows of files, all labeled by the year.

"I photographed only about six or seven girls a year from the year I arrived here until Cathy and I turned our attention to our business and I dropped the photography for a while."

Pickett could see that he had kept good records and she was surprised they had survived so long. But it made sense considering how well known he was for his art.

"Can we look at the March house files," Cavanaugh said. "Once you and Cathy were together?"

Ben nodded and pulled out 1977. "It was Cathy and her natural blonde hair that got me interested in blondes and a book came out of it that started to make my reputation as an artist, actually. Although I didn't take advantage of it until almost a decade later."

He handed Cavanaugh the file and left the room, coming back a moment later with a large photo book of nudes. The title was just *Blondes*. He handed that to Pickett.

"Some of the women, if I remember right, from the 1977 March house are in that book," Ben said.

Pickett opened the book. It was heavy and very well done. The copyright was 1981. The book's dedication was "To my beautiful wife Cathy."

Pickett was impressed. All the women were blonde, all the photos were art photos, very well done, very tastefully posed.

And about half of the backgrounds were regular bedrooms like the ones in those horror homes.

Pickett leafed through it, then handed it to Sarge, who did the same.

"So these are the names and addresses of the six women you photographed that year in the March house. Correct?" Cavanaugh asked.

Ben glanced at the folder that Cavanaugh had, then said, "Yes, that is correct."

"Would you mind if I give these names to another detective?" Cavanaugh asked. "Again, we will do our best to keep these completely confidential."

"If it helps with this, please," Ben said.

Pickett watched as Sarge called Robin, then clicked pictures of the files and sent them to her. Then he hung up.

Knowing Robin, they would know more about those girls very shortly.

Pickett watched as Cavanaugh took out the 1978 file and looked at it.

"Anything more you can tell us about Cathy's family?" Pickett asked of Ben. "Her father, brother, anything that might help us on this?"

"Her father was one sick son-of-a-bitch," Ben said, clear coldness in his voice. "I only met him twice and didn't like him. When Cathy first told me what he was doing to her and her mother, I wanted to go kill him. Cathy made me not do that."

"Smart woman," Sarge said.

Ben just nodded. Pickett could tell that Ben wasn't convinced that was the right decision yet.

"Did she know who you actually were by that point?" Pickett asked.

"Yes," Ben said. "The moment we started falling in love, I told her the complete truth. And that was when I started learning about her father as well."

"And you never thought to check on him after you two left?" Sarge asked.

"Never," Ben said. "Cathy and I thought we had escaped. Our focus was to put that behind us. Cathy only felt bad about leaving her little brother in there, but we had no real choice. He was only five and she knew her father and mother had no interest in boys at all. Only girls in their sick games around death. So we figured he would be all right. Another reason to not look and check on what they were doing. We just didn't want to know."

Pickett understood that. She hadn't really checked on her ex-husband who left her for an overblown chest because she just didn't want to know.

Cavanaugh's phone buzzed and he answered it with a "Yes."

Pickett watched as he listened for a moment. She knew he was talking with Robin. She had no idea how much of what Robin was telling him he would decide to share with Ben.

And since this was Cavanaugh's case, that was his decision.

After a moment Cavanaugh said, "I will check."

Cavanaugh turned to Ben. "May I send the names for the next six or seven years as well? It is going to take some time to research all these since so many years have passed and we don't want to bother you and Cathy again if we can help it."

Pickett nodded to Sarge. Cavanaugh was very slick. He had decided to not tell Ben anything more.

Ben said, "Sure, go ahead."

He opened up the files for Cavanaugh.

"Photos of the other years coming through now," Cavanaugh said.

Then with Ben helping, Cavanaugh took a photo of each page with the girls' names and information and model releases and sent it to Robin.

They got to 1982 and Ben said, "The blonde project was over by this point and I only did one shoot. And none for the next four years after that."

Cavanaugh nodded, took the one last picture of the records from 1982, checked with Robin that she got them all, then hung up.

"Thank you," Cavanaugh said, reaching out to Ben and shaking his hand as he stood. "And apologize to Cathy for us for upsetting her."

Pickett and Sarge followed Cavanaugh's lead, thanking Ben and heading toward the front door.

Cavanaugh handed Ben a card. "Please, if you can think of anything more you might know, call me at any point."

"We will," Ben said. "I am sure this will be a topic of conversation for us for the first time in a decade."

"I am sorry about that," Cavanaugh said.

"Detectives, please don't be sorry," Ben said. "You are only doing your jobs."

Five minutes later Pickett had then headed down the long driveway from the beautiful home. They were headed for lunch at the Bellagio Café. Cavanaugh was following them in his car.

It seems they had made progress.

And slid backward at the same time.

Robin was going to meet them for lunch, and Pickett had a hunch Robin knew who the victims were now.

And as sad as that was, it actually was progress.

But they still didn't know who the killer was or what was actually going on in those six houses of horror.

CHAPTER TWENTY-TWO

June 15th, 2017
Las Vegas, Nevada

Sarge and Pickett got to the Bellagio Café before both Robin and Cavanaugh. They managed to get a waiter to clear off their favorite booth from a group that had it before them. The sounds of the casino felt normal and the smell of the food calmed Sarge. The conversation this morning was anything but calming, that was for sure.

As they got seated, Cavanaugh joined them.

Sarge watched the detective sort of slow-walk his way toward the table through the crowded restaurant. Cavanaugh was an amazing man and an amazing detective. The regular force was going to miss him, but the Cold Poker Gang were all going to welcome him with open arms.

"Well, this is a sick mess," Cavanaugh said as he slid into the booth.

"They didn't clean off your side of the table there or something?" Pickett asked, pretending to be serious.

Cavanaugh actually snorted.

"Thank you," he said, winking at her. "I needed that."

Pickett and Sarge had talked about the case on the way into town. The fact that the houses actually had regular visitors just recently might just help them. More than likely that sort of thing was set up over the dark web, but Robin and her people were really good at tracing damn near anything.

"The depravity of the human animal, especially in this town, never ceases to amaze me," Sarge said.

"As old and jaded as we are as detectives," Pickett said, "you think we would be used to anything."

"Speak for yourself about the old part," Cavanaugh said, smiling at her. "I have fifteen days before I become officially old."

"Noted," Pickett said, smiling.

"So what did you two think of old Ben and Cathy?" Cavanaugh asked.

"I think Cathy was an abuse victim," Pickett said. "Seen a lot of that over the years and she sure didn't seem to be faking any of those reactions, although I could be wrong on that."

"Agreed," Sarge said. "And Ben seems to be, on the surface, a really good guy who rescued the woman he loved. And they have been a team ever since."

Sarge worried about that reaction. It wasn't normal for him to have a suspect he completely believed. It had happened, but rarely. It happened again today with Ben and Cathy.

"Think it a little weird that Cathy helped him with his nude photography?" Cavanaugh asked. "After all that happened with her and her father and mother?"

"No," Pickett said, shaking her head. "The photography

wasn't about sex, it was about fun and art. Remember how happy all those women in those pictures were? Cathy made being naked natural and fun and alive for the woman, not something twisted and ugly and dead like her father had done."

Cavanaugh nodded.

"So Robin knew who some of the victims are?" Sarge asked.

"Yup," Cavanaugh said. "No point in telling Ben about the other stuff, especially about what happened to his models because he photographed them. With luck, he will never learn that part. Bad enough they were killed because he and Cathy had photographed them."

Sarge agreed. It was going to be hard enough when Ben completely realized that someone targeted the women he found, the ones he put in his book, and then had killed them. Ben and Cathy didn't need the rest of it.

"Are we missing something here?" Sarge asked, suddenly realizing that he had looked at a book full of nudes from a professional photographer. "There are a lot of nut jobs out there who might hate what Ben was doing with the nudes."

"Some religious zealot who thinks nudity is a sin and the sinner should be punished?" Cavanaugh asked, nodding. "Maybe."

"We could even have a sick boyfriend of one of the girls be our killer," Pickett said.

"So our suspect pool just grew," Cavanaugh said, shaking his head. "Wonderful, just wonderful."

Sarge felt exactly the same way. They needed to narrow the suspects, not increase them.

CHAPTER TWENTY-THREE

June 15th, 2017
Las Vegas, Nevada

Pickett watched as Robin wound her way through the tables of the Bellagio Café toward them. She had a backpack over her shoulder which meant she was carrying a lot of information and her computer.

Robin joined them. "Ain't this case a pile of joy?"

"Sick doesn't even start to describe it," Pickett said.

Everyone nodded.

"So do we now know who all the victims are?" Sarge asked.

"All but three of the thirty-one," Robin said. "They didn't disappear the year that States did his photography shoot. In fact, they all disappeared in 1981 and were killed and embalmed that year."

"After the fire at his dark room office," Pickett said.

Robin nodded. "It was a pretty extreme missing person's

year that year and had a police task force set up on the cases, but without luck."

"Eighty-one was the last year Ben owned one of those houses, right?" Cavanaugh asked.

"Yes," Robin said. "And the last year the crematorium existed out off the old highway."

"So the timeline all fits," Pickett said. "If we can assume that Cathy's father was doing this, he was trying to destroy Ben and Cathy by putting all the bodies up in the attics in homes they owned."

"Looks that way," Robin said. "At least that's one theory. I have no other at the moment, to be honest."

Pickett had her notebook open and went to a couple questions she had.

"How did Cathy's father manage to keep Ben's fake name on the title when he bought it?"

"I don't know yet," Robin said.

"He just had a fake broker send fake paperwork to Ben," Cavanaugh said, "and the money and have him sign. The house never really transferred, although Ben thought it did and got paid for it."

Pickett looked at Cavanaugh and the detective shrugged. "Worked a scam case back about fifteen years ago where that was the scam. Only the buyers were getting drug houses to use, leaving the original owners holding the bag."

Sarge shook his head. "A great way to get storage. The guy putting the bodies up in the attic was getting the money for the houses from the bodies."

"How much were they paying the crematorium for each cremation?"

"Nine hundred a body," Robin said. "Some more, but nine hundred was the minimum at that time."

"For a hundred bodies a house," Sarge said, "that's ninety grand. Wow. What did that house sell for back then?"

"Twenty-three thousand," Robin said, glancing at her notes.

Pickett was stunned. The money explained a lot of this.

At that moment the waiter came to take their order.

They all four ordered lunches and iced teas, then after the waiter left, Robin said, "Want the real disgusting stuff now?"

Pickett shook her head no.

"Do we have to?" Sarge asked.

"Getting old is making these two whiners, isn't it?" Cavanaugh asked Robin.

"No," Robin said, smiling, "they just know when I say something is disgusting, it is really disgusting."

"Now I don't want to hear it either," Cavanaugh said.

"Too late," Pickett said, laughing. "She's going to tell us anyway."

Robin nodded and dug out some notes.

"I called a friend at the lab who was working on this case and she and I decided to focus in on just one body in the second house that was in the bed upstairs."

Pickett nodded. "I told you about how the body was embalmed with the genitals sewn open? From what my friend can tell, the body was 'cleaned out' every few months or so for the entire thirty-five years since the poor woman was killed and embalmed."

"Oh, my god," Cavanaugh said, shaking his head.

"So we only have DNA traces for the last five or six uses of the corpse."

"Five or six uses in three months?"

Robin nodded. "That was just one body."

"So why did they bury some of the girls," Sarge asked, "if they were being used?"

"Burying didn't stop the use," Robin said. "Each basement had a shovel in it and each body had been buried in a very shallow grave in a black tarp that the forensics are getting prints off of. A lot of prints. Seems the girls were being dug up and reburied all the time."

Pickett just sort of shuddered. This really was disgusting. Robin had been right.

"Are you telling me that a guy could go in there, dig up a girl and have sex with her?" Cavanaugh asked.

Robin nodded. "I found the listings for the houses on the dark web. The listings have not been updated and are not responding. But yes, exactly that."

"Any way to trace those listings?"

"Will has his best working on it," Robin said. "Trying to come at it from the contact side. But looks as if the clientele of these houses were from all over the world. And they paid $5,000 for two days' rental of the house. Unlimited use of the facilities."

Pickett just shook her head and tried not to imagine any of it.

Sarge looked at the stunned face of Cavanaugh. "I warned you about when Robin says something is disgusting, don't ask."

Cavanaugh laughed. "That's some pretty sick shit."

"Very sick," Pickett said. "Very damned sick."

CHAPTER TWENTY-FOUR

June 15th, 2017
Las Vegas, Nevada

They ate their lunches and talked about other things beside the case, which Sarge was very happy to do at this point. This case was not one that made eating easy, and he had eaten at some pretty nasty crime scenes.

But something about abusing the corpse of a young woman for thirty-five years just made him sick and want to punch someone. Any of the sick bastards who used those houses would do.

Sarge hoped that the families of all those girls would never know what their daughter's body had ever gone through after death. Just no point at all in telling them.

After they got done with lunch and were just talking, the conversation came back to the case.

"So we are going to close thirty-one missing person's cold cases," Pickett said.

"Thirty-two," Robin said, "counting Cathy and Ben."

"Forgot about that one," Pickett said. "The one that started all this."

"So how do we figure out who Cathy's brother's father was, the guy in that basement?" Sarge asked. "The brother flat didn't want to cooperate much at all when we talked to him about Cathy."

Cavanaugh shrugged. "How about we go see him and I threaten to take him downtown and question him for murder if he doesn't talk."

Sarge laughed. "He was only nine or ten in 1981."

"We won't tell him which murders," Cavanaugh said. "And we can get him if he withholds information as well if we want."

"Can't hurt," Pickett said and Sarge agreed.

"I'm headed back to see if Will and his people have managed any forward motion from the computer side and then help on the scanning of fingerprints from the tarps and shovels and other places in those houses. If we find one of the creeps and threaten to expose him, he might roll on the people who ran the operation."

Sarge really liked that idea.

"I want to be the one to question the guy," Cavanaugh said, "preferably in a dark alley with a dumpster nearby."

Pickett laughed. Then raised her hand. "Can I help?"

"I am going to be so happy when you join the gang," Sarge said to Cavanaugh.

Robin nodded as she gathered up her stuff and put it back in her pack. "You certainly fit with this bunch, that's for sure."

Cavanaugh only shrugged. "Fifteen days. And then someone else gets to do the rest of the paperwork on this mess."

Cavanaugh decided to leave his car at the Bellagio and ride with Pickett and Sarge out the Strip to where Kevin Wendt worked. They knew he was on duty, so they were just going to surprise him.

They found Kevin just as he was coming off his shift, and Cavanaugh flashed his badge and said they needed to talk.

Kevin was a short guy, not more than five-three, and wore lift boots to make him seem a little taller. He had dark black hair, dark eyes, and a chin that didn't seem to exist at times. He wore the standard dealer's blue shirt, dark vest, and dark slacks.

From what Robin had found out about him, he had been married once and divorced and lived in an apartment within walking distance of his job. He had been dealing blackjack now for eleven years and had a clean reputation at work.

He had no debts, but few bills, and didn't seem to spend much money at all. He seemed to be just surviving, which was the opinion Sarge had left with when they talked with him the first time.

Angry surviving, but surviving.

They showed their badges and got off the casino floor and back into a meeting room.

"Still looking for my long-dead sister?" Kevin asked as he dropped down into a chair and let the others take a seat around the Formica table.

There was a projector screen on one wall at the end of the table and a dozen chairs around the table. Some work posters covered another wall. Otherwise this was just a regular, plain meeting room like Sarge had seen a hundred times over the years, plain, dull, without a window and only one wooden door.

"Her case has expanded some," Cavanaugh said. "And we think your father is involved."

"That sick bastard vanished in 1981 when I was twelve and mom had become useless to his sex games."

Sarge was stunned that Kevin knew about those and admitted it. That did not bode well.

"Not that father," Cavanaugh said. "Your biological father."

Kevin did not react as Sarge had expected him to act. Instead Kevin's eyes got cold and he said, "How did you know about him?"

"DNA," Cavanaugh said. "We found his body at the scene of a pretty major crime. And we think you might be involved as well."

Kevin sat back. "I'm not involved with anything. So he's dead?"

Cavanaugh nodded.

Sarge had a hunch that Kevin knew he was dead.

Kevin clearly didn't seem to care one way or another about the news.

"What can you tell us about him?" Cavanaugh asked. "His name, where he lived, that sort of thing?"

"Don't know much," Kevin said. "His name was Douglas Trueman and he and my father went into some business together back before my dad vanished. After my dad left, dear old Doug tried to take up with my mom. He even lived with us for a while, but my mother was pretty broken. She told me one day when we were alone that Douglas was my real father."

Sarge nodded to that.

"As I told the other detectives here, my mother killed herself when I was sixteen and good old Douglas vanished as well, leaving me to clean up the mess, sell my parents house and things, and be on my own. Never saw the bastard again and never want to. Glad they are all gone, actually. I'm starting to get some counseling finally and might actually be able to do a little something before I get too old."

Sarge had no idea if the guy was lying or not, but it was a

convincing story. A story he would have been expected to tell. At least they had a name they could go on for that body in the basement.

"So what's this crime you are suspecting me of being involved with?" Kevin asked.

"We weren't sure if you were involved with your biological father or not," Cavanaugh said. "Sounds like you were not."

"Never saw the guy again after mom died," Kevin said, shrugging. "Never cared to, either."

"Do you know if Douglas had any other family at all?" Cavanaugh asked, glancing at his notes.

Kevin shook his head. "Nope. Not a clue."

They thanked him and they headed back through the hallway and into the noise of the casino.

On the way out, Pickett said, "Cavanaugh, you didn't hear this."

"Hear what?" Cavanaugh asked.

"Exactly," Pickett said as she took out her phone and called Robin.

"We just left Kevin and I cloned his phone," Pickett said to Robin. "Sending it to you now. We rattled his cage pretty well, so if he's involved, he's going to be making some calls."

Pickett nodded and clicked off her phone.

"She's got it."

"You know that I am pretty sure that's illegal," Cavanaugh said, laughing as they got to the front of the casino to get their car from valet parking.

"So is doing what those perverts did to those girls for the last thirty-five years," Pickett said. "Not counting the murders in the first place."

Sarge laughed and patted Cavanaugh on the back. "Don't

worry, if anything comes of it, we'll back it up with a legal path to the information."

Cavanaugh laughed as well. "I know. Just enjoying watching you three work is all. No wonder you figure out so many cases."

"We cheat," Pickett said.

"No," Sarge said, "we use modern resources."

"Actually," Cavanaugh said, "you are smarter than the crooks."

"I think I'll take that as a compliment," Sarge said, laughing.

"Don't let it go to your head," Cavanaugh said.

CHAPTER TWENTY-FIVE

June 15th, 2017
Las Vegas, Nevada

Pickett was fifty-fifty on the odds that Kevin was involved. Part of her wanted him to not be, but part of her knew that the fruit didn't fall far from the tree. And his answers were too pat and expected.

And he had been sixteen when his mother killed herself. He had been old enough to participate in his father's habits and who knows, as a strong boy, what he was forcing his mother to do. Nothing was going to surprise Pickett anymore about this case.

The three of them talked about the theory that Douglas Trueman, if that was his real name, had murdered Cathy Wendt's real father in 1981, when he vanished.

But if he had been dead, who killed those girls and why?

So Pickett was conflicted about that as well. None of them

were sure that Cathy Wendt's real father just didn't change his name and keep going.

And he might be alive out there somewhere now.

The afternoon had grown hot when they pulled back up beside Cavanaugh's car in the Bellagio's main parking lot. Right at that moment, Robin called them.

Pickett put it on speakerphone and told Robin that all three of them were still here.

"This gets worse," Robin said.

"I really, really wish you would stop saying that," Cavanaugh said.

"I found Cathy's real father, I think," Robin said. "Kevin called him as soon as you guys left him. The guy's going under the name of Craig C. Verne and he's the right age. We are still digging, but I think he worked as an embalmer from 1999 to 2001. He was licensed. Then he retired, only working those two years. Made a lot of money from somewhere and is still making money."

"Can you get into Kevin's computers and such?" Pickett asked.

"Going to need a warrant for Will and me and our people to try that," Robin said. "The guy might be protected from all sides since the dark web stuff these places were doing was very upscale."

Cavanaugh nodded, then said, "I'll have one for you in thirty minutes. Need a solid reason why, however."

"Suspicion of involvement with twenty-four murders," Robin said.

"Not all thirty-one?" Pickett asked.

Sarge just shook his head.

"Don't say it," Cavanaugh said from the back seat.

"Sorry," Robin said, "but there is another pattern of twenty-four girls going missing, eighteen years old to twenty-two. All brunettes this time, all thin and beautiful. All during the two years that Verne worked as an embalmer."

"Find the goddamned houses they are using," Cavanaugh said. "I'll have the warrant to you as fast as I can."

Pickett had jumped to the exact same conclusion. There were more of these houses out there with dead girls in them. Robin had been right about this getting worse.

A whole bunch worse.

"Will do," Robin said and hung up.

"What do you want us to do?" Pickett asked as Cavanaugh started to climb out.

"Get some rest for the afternoon, some good dinner," Cavanaugh said.

"So we're going out tonight?" Sarge asked.

"It's a date," Cavanaugh said. "Only no dancing. You remember stakeouts from your time on the active list? Or do I need to explain them to you?"

Pickett laughed. She remembered them well. Never had liked them, but oh, did she remember the many nights she and Robin had spent on stakeouts.

"We'll use this car," Cavanaugh said. "Might want to toss some pillows and blankets in here and in the back so we can take turns napping."

"Will do," Pickett said.

Cavanaugh got out, his phone against his ear before he even closed the door.

"Any idea who we are going to be staking out?" Pickett asked.

Sarge just shrugged. "Got a hunch that will depend on what Robin finds with those warrants."

Pickett knew that was right.

"Our first stakeout together," Sarge said, smiling at Pickett.

"Too bad we're going to have a chaperone," Pickett said.

"Well, detective, I am shocked at the very suggestion," Sarge said, laughing.

"I'm shocked you didn't suggest it," Pickett said, getting the car in motion.

"Maybe we can get Cavanaugh to take a break for dinner," Sarge said.

"Now that idea I like," Pickett said.

She would have kissed the man she loved at that moment, but she was already driving.

PART FOUR

Disappointing

CHAPTER TWENTY-SIX

June 15th, 2017
Las Vegas, Nevada

Sarge was feeling full, but not full enough to stay away from seconds.

That afternoon, he and Pickett had gone home, taken a long nap together, then they had showered and put on their most comfortable clothes for the possibly long night ahead. Both had on jeans, light shirts, and tennis shoes.

They both had grabbed light coats as well as the jackets they normally wore over the guns and badges, just in case the night got really cold, which it often did, even in the early summer.

They had filled up the car with gas, bought a bunch of snacks for the night, and filled the cooler with bottles of iced tea and coffee drinks, as well as water and juices.

While they were doing that, they both told their worst stakeout stories. Both of them hoped tonight would not rank in the even memorable ones, except maybe that it would be their very last. Stakeouts were for active detectives, not retired detectives.

In most cases.

Then they had headed to the Golden Nugget buffet just because it was easy and comfortable and they could wait there until pretty late for Cavanaugh to call.

By the time they got there the dinner rush was over and most of the tourists were on one side of the restaurant by the pool windows. Sarge and Pickett got their normal table clear on the other side of the restaurant and settled in.

The light in there at night was very different from morning. It had a golden glow to it in the seating areas because of large wooden-framed chandeliers, with white light around the buffet area making the area seem like the Promised Land.

Sarge had just finished his first plate of salad and prime rib and some shrimp when Robin called.

Since they were far enough away from any occupied table or server, they put her on speakerphone, turned the sound down a little, and leaned in so they could both hear.

"Both here," Pickett said. "Finishing dinner at the Nugget."

"You two ever get tired of that place?" Robin asked, laughing.

"Tough to get tired of great food, comfortable seating, and nice wait staff," Sarge said.

"Got a point there," Robin said. "Well, we got a hit on about six sets of fingerprints of the customers in the houses. We are pretty sure they are customers because they all live on the East Coast. Two work in the Federal government, which is why we found their prints."

Sarge just shook his head and hoped the worst for them.

Robin went on. "You will never guess who owns five more

houses similar to the ones we found earlier in style and shape," Robin said. "Our dear old Ben."

Sarge sat back and looked at Pickett, who looked as surprised as he felt.

"Any direct connection this time?" Pickett asked.

"Again, nothing," Robin said. "He bought them all in 1998, sold them in 1999."

"Did you track Ben's broker on those?" Sarge asked.

"Guy is dead, company out of business since 2005," Robin said. "I pulled up the paperwork that was filed and it looks fine, only the house sales were never finalized and transferred out of Ben's name. Just as the other six."

"Could he be doing this to protect himself?" Sarge asked.

He had believed Ben and Cathy. But that doesn't mean he hadn't been wrong.

"He might be," Robin said. "But I have dug into their accounts, including five corporations they own and control. All money seems to be aboveboard. If they are involved, they are not doing it for the money. Or the money is going somewhere I can't yet find, some off-shore corporation or something."

"So we have found the houses?" Pickett asked.

"Cavanaugh has detectives on all five of them," Robin said. "But we don't want to move on any of them until we find the people behind this sickness and murders."

Sarge suddenly had an idea that had not occurred to him, since before they were dealing with very old houses. But if they were correct and these new houses fired up at the start of this century, they might have some technology in them.

"Robin," Sarge said. "Any way you can get a scan to catch any kind of remote signal coming out of those houses? Like secret taping or monitoring devices broadcasting a signal?"

"Shit," Robin said. "Great idea. "Call you back after I get that going. Not sure why I didn't think of that. Shit."

She hung up.

Pickett smiled at him and pointed to the dessert area of the buffet.

"Nope, not yet. Got a hunch we have time, so I'm going for some more shrimp and a slice of that ham."

Pickett followed him and got a slice of prime rib and some melon balls for her seconds.

And he had been right, they had more than enough time to have seconds, drink a cup of coffee, and get some dessert.

CHAPTER TWENTY-SEVEN

June 15th, 2017
Las Vegas, Nevada

It was just after nine in the evening when Robin called back. Most of the buffet was empty and it would close at ten. So Pickett was glad that they still had a little time and their waitress had told them they could stay as long as they wanted, the kitchen staff just had to clean up the food at ten.

Pickett figured it was better sitting here than in a car any longer than they had to.

Pickett put Robin on speakerphone again.

"Cavanaugh got a surveillance warrant for all five houses," Robin said, "and Will has his people set up on all five. They are getting some pretty nasty stuff from four of the five houses, from what Will tells me."

"Sick stuff?" Pickett asked, afraid of the answer.

"Real sick," Robin said. "I warned Will what might be going

on. He said he thinks he can keep his people from killing anyone in the house. But after a few minutes they all have stopped watching the feed. They are just recording it."

Pickett understood that perfectly and Sarge just nodded. Her imagination was more than enough to imagine the horror in those houses. She certainly didn't want to see it.

"We are making progress on cracking the web side of this," Robin said. "Pretty clear it is coming from Kevin."

Pickett wasn't surprised at that at all.

"So got any idea why Cavanaugh wants us on this stakeout tonight?" Sarge asked.

"Because he believes," Robin said, "that everyone involved is about ready to cut and run since we have gotten this close. And he hopes to wrap this up before the rats scatter to the trash heaps."

"You got both the father and son locked down, right?" Pickett said.

"They are meeting at midnight tonight." Robin said. "We have trackers on their cars and both of their phones cloned. You shook the kid's tree nicely this afternoon."

Pickett smiled. "That was all Cavanaugh. He can do that to a person if he wants. And in a nice way while at it."

Robin laughed, then went on. "We also just learned about thirty minutes ago from the lab that the guy in the basement, Kevin's biological father, didn't die of natural causes and dehydration. He was poisoned."

That surprised Pickett. The guy just looked like he had sat there and died. They were such a long way in this case from how they started when they saw that body the first time.

"So they cut those early six houses and were waiting for them to be discovered is all," Sarge said. "We just happened to stumble into it all."

"Seems that way," Robin said.

"What wonderful luck," Pickett said.

"Yeah, luck," Sarge said, shaking his head.

"But there is someone else involved, isn't there?" Pickett asked Robin.

"We don't know for sure," Robin said. "But Cavanaugh is guessing that Ben and Cathy are. So he wants you three sitting on them tonight."

Pickett glanced up at the puzzled look on Sarge's face. Then she asked, "What makes Cavanaugh think that?"

"First off, your idea about the cars. We matched a few cash withdrawals from Ben and Cathy's personal accounts for travel to the price of the cars when they were bought. Seems the cars were never used, just put there for show."

"Extremely circumstantial," Pickett said. "But makes sense."

She didn't like it, but it made sense to compare across like that.

"The coincidence of the new five houses being in Ben's name," Robin said, "is another factor. And he did another book of nudes in 2000 called *Brunettes*. Seems like too pat a story to not be checked out."

"I agree," Pickett said. "But I sure hope we are wrong."

"I hope so too," Sarge said. "But the cycle of abuse tends to go down through the generations until broken. We all know that."

"Oh, god, tell me Ben and Cathy had no children," Pickett said. "And Kevin has no children."

"They had no children," Robin said.

Pickett was relieved to hear that. No matter what happened tonight, that chain of sickness was broken. Now she just hoped that Cathy and Ben were not a part of all this.

But it was only a hope.

She had nothing else to go on because their story said things were one way, but the facts seemed to be pushing another.

It was going to be a long night.

CHAPTER TWENTY-EIGHT

June 15th, 2017
Las Vegas, Nevada

Cavanaugh had met them in a twenty-four-hour grocery store parking lot about a block from one of the houses being staked out. It was ten in the evening and he looked actually cheerful as he got out of his car and locked it and climbed into the back of Pickett's SUV.

Sarge glanced at Pickett, who was behind the wheel, and then turned around to Cavanaugh. "Too much caffeine?"

Cavanaugh laughed. "Nope, by tomorrow we'll have this sick case wrapped up and I will only have fourteen days left."

Pickett and Sarge both laughed.

"So where to?" Pickett asked.

"There is a service station about three-quarters of a mile below Cathy and Ben's house, on that crossroads there. They are open twenty-four seven and we can park beside it without being seen much from the highway."

"What happens if they go another way out of the house on the highway?"

"I got a guy with a scope on their garage and driveway," Cavanaugh said. "We'll track them if they leave."

Pickett got the car headed out toward Ben and Cathy's place.

"You believe they are involved?"

"I'm damn hoping not," Cavanaugh said. "But her dad and her brother are meeting tonight at midnight in the one house that is not being used by a customer at the moment. We think this is either a normal meeting or a called meeting."

"Robin or Will or their crew find any sign that either the father or the brother had contacted Ben or Cathy in any way?"

"No," Cavanaugh said. "That's what gives me hope. Unless this is just a regular meeting. On the dark web booking of this stuff, Will's people discovered that two nights a month are left reserved in one house or another. Tonight is one of those nights."

"So we have no idea at all if Ben and Cathy are involved," Sarge said.

"Not a bit that will stand up in any court," Cavanaugh said. "But no matter if Ben and Cathy come out or not, this operation stops tonight. And we toss everyone we can round up into general population and pass the word about exactly what they were doing."

Sarge really liked that idea.

Pickett just laughed, and Sarge could tell she liked it as well.

Thirty minutes later Pickett got the SUV backed into a place in the shadows of the service station lighting, against one side of the building and to the back. They had a clear view of the highway in both directions from there, but Sarge was pretty sure the car didn't look obvious in any way.

"This is stakeout heaven," Pickett said. "Hot coffee in there, bathrooms on the other side of the building."

"We are too damned old to do a regular stakeout," Cavanaugh said.

"I thought you said you weren't old yet," Sarge said.

Cavanaugh waved his hand in dismissal. "I'm just watching out for my senior friends is all."

Pickett actually laughed and Sarge just shook his head. Actually, in real age, Pickett was younger than both he and Cavanaugh.

"I'm going to go tell the guy behind the counter we are here," Cavanaugh said, "so we don't spook him."

"What's the cover story?" Sarge asked.

"Watching for a truckload of stolen watches coming down from the north," Cavanaugh said.

Sarge laughed at that. Maybe this wasn't going to be such a long night after all.

CHAPTER TWENTY-NINE

June 15th, 2017
Las Vegas, Nevada

All three of them were munching on some rather tasty fresh donuts that had just been delivered to the service station. Pickett had her favorite, a maple bar, covered completely in maple and still slightly warm, with the maple frosting running so that she had more of it on her face than in her mouth after the first bite.

But she didn't care. It tasted heavenly.

Fresh donuts on a stakeout always did.

It was eleven thirty and they had been there for over an hour and were just getting settled in. They had all decided that the outcome they wanted was to sit there until just before dawn and then go in and help in the raid on those homes.

They had all clearly liked Cathy and Ben.

Suddenly the two-way radio Cavanaugh had with him crackled to life.

"White Lexus SUV pulling out of the garage and heading down the driveway."

"Shit, shit, shit," Cavanaugh said.

Pickett felt exactly the same way.

Sarge just sat shaking his head.

"Tell us which way it turns on the main highway," Cavanaugh said to his spotter.

"Copy," the spotter said.

"And stay in place until dawn, make sure a second car doesn't leave."

"Understood," the cop on the other side said.

Pickett had so hoped that Ben and Cathy were not involved. But it was looking like they were. Or at least Ben was.

She cleaned up her hands and face and put what was left of her maple bar in a bag with Sarge's half-eaten glazed donut.

Sarge put the bag on the floor at his feet.

"Turning toward you on the highway," the spotter said. "White Lexus and I only see one person inside."

"Understood," Cavanaugh said. "We'll pick it up from here."

He then radioed into dispatch that he was going to need some backup on a tail of a white Lexus.

Then they sat in silence, waiting.

"Here it comes," Sarge said.

As the Lexus went by in front of them in the lights from the service station, it was clear who was driving.

Cathy.

Not Ben.

Cathy.

And from what Pickett could tell, it didn't look like Ben was in the car with her.

"Well ain't that a kick," Cavanaugh said as Pickett waited a moment for Cathy to get far enough past, then started up her car and pulled out on the highway.

Pickett wasn't sure what she thought. One thing was for sure, that was not what she had hoped for.

But she knew, knowing just a little of the abuse that Cathy had suffered, it was what she should have expected.

PART FIVE

Unexpected But No Surprise

CHAPTER THIRTY

June 15th, 2017
Las Vegas, Nevada

Sarge sat in the passenger seat, helping Pickett keep an eye on the white Lexus a quarter mile in front of them.

Two other unmarked police spotters were leapfrogging them, keeping them informed on a private channel of the location of the Lexus.

They rode in a heavy quiet, almost like it was a funeral. Sarge knew they were all hoping that Cathy would just pull into a grocery store, get some medicine or food and head home.

Sarge knew that was what he was hoping for at least.

None of them wanted her to go to that house with the dead girls on the beds and two buried in the basement.

But after all the years on the force, his detective mind told him he was just kidding himself. Cathy was going right where they knew she was going.

It was clear now that almost from the start in 1977 as a

young girl, she had played Ben and helped her father and her brother's father get rich off of not cremating dead people. Then, in 1981, they had killed those girls and set up an entire new business.

And then killed another group in 2001.

Clearly tonight was not a special meeting, but a normal one of the three of them.

"Both men are en route," a dispatcher said to Cavanaugh.

"Make sure all surveillance vehicles on the house are pulled back and out of sight," Cavanaugh said.

"So what's the plan?" Pickett asked of Cavanaugh as Cathy turned toward the house.

"We let all three get inside," Cavanaugh said. "We have the house completely monitored, so as soon as we get enough information from them, we go in and shut it down."

"You have teams on the other four houses?" Sarge asked.

Cavanaugh nodded. "Ready for my signal. In three of them there is a single guy, in another there is a couple from Indiana."

"A couple?" Pickett asked, glancing back at Cavanaugh.

"Afraid so," Cavanaugh said, clearly sounding disgusted.

"How in the hell does a couple bond over sexually abusing long-dead corpses?" Sarge asked, feeling like he wanted to be just sick.

"They met at a funeral?" Pickett asked. "Standing over the corpse viewing. A real romance meet cute if you ask me."

Sarge shook his head and smiled.

Cavanaugh chuckled.

"Maybe they both like to pretend to be vampires," Cavanaugh said. "I hear kids like that sort of thing these days."

"Pretty sure mummified dead bodies don't have blood," Pickett said, laughing.

"Can you imagine the dinner conversations?" Sarge asked. "Honey, you up for some necrophilia this weekend?"

Cavanaugh snorted.

"What would foreplay be like?" Pickett asked. "You play dead so I can get warmed up?"

All three of them laughed and Sarge waved his hand to stop the conversation.

At that point Pickett pulled over into a driveway of a neighbor's house about a block away and shut off the car and lights.

"Suspect you were following is entering the building," Cavanaugh's radio reported.

"Both other suspects have just pulled up in front."

A minute later the report came in. "All three suspects are in the building."

"Shall we go to the surveillance van?" Sarge said.

Sarge was not at all sure he wanted to and he could see that Pickett didn't want to either.

He was about to say no when the spotter on the States' home said, "Cavanaugh, another car is leaving the garage. A second white Lexus SUV."

"What the hell is Ben doing?" Sarge asked.

"Damn it," Cavanaugh said.

"We'll go back and pick him up," Pickett said. "You take care of this mess here."

Cavanaugh reported back to the spotter that he needed to report which way the Lexus was headed out of the driveway. Then he called in to headquarters the situation and that they had undercover officers who would be tailing the Lexus and who would need help.

Headquarters responded back in the affirmative and

Cavanaugh handed Sarge his radio. "I'll be monitoring the situation from here."

He climbed out and Pickett got the car headed back toward the States' house.

"What in the world is Ben doing?" Pickett asked.

"Maybe they both are involved," Sarge said. "No way of knowing."

"Get Robin on the phone, tell her what is happening," Pickett said. "We might need her to track Ben's car if we lose him."

Sarge nodded, put Cavanaugh's radio between his legs and called Robin on the phone. He put her on speakerphone and they filled her in on what was happening.

"Nothing is going on at the moment in the house," Robin said. "I am getting the live feed just as the police are. They are all sitting in the living room talking. Like a board of director's meeting or something."

Sarge just shook his head. In that house there were three girls in three beds, all dead since 2001. The mummified bodies embalmed and adjusted for sex. And two other girls were buried in the basement, ready to be dug up for sex. And those three just sat in the living room talking.

"Can you hear what they are saying?"

"She is telling them about your visit," Robin said. "She is laughing at you guys for being fooled."

Sarge looked at Pickett as she was driving. The woman he loved looked angry.

Very angry.

And he felt the same way.

"Detectives," the spotter Cavanaugh had watching the States' home said.

"Go ahead," Sarge said.

"The second Lexus turned toward town as well. One person inside."

"Thank you," Sarge said. "Stay in position."

"Understand, sir," the spotter said.

Sarge then said, "Cavanaugh."

"Go ahead," Cavanaugh said.

"We're going to try to intercept the second Lexus about three miles in on the highway and will follow it."

"Understood," Cavanaugh said.

"First time in a long time that I wished I had police lights on this thing," Pickett said.

Sarge laughed. "Chief gave us our guns and badges. Let's don't go hoping for too much."

She laughed, but never took her eyes off the road as she expertly worked her way through traffic, not even really speeding.

She was a great driver. Of that there was no doubt.

CHAPTER THIRTY-ONE

June 16th, 2017
Las Vegas, Nevada

It was only a few minutes after midnight as Pickett swung across the highway into a convenience store parking lot and turned the car quickly around.

If she had timed it right and the second Lexus hadn't turned off, it would be passing this point in about one minute.

If he had turned off, it was going to take luck and some of Robin's skills to find it.

While they had been driving, Robin had been not only reporting a little on the meeting in the house over Sarge's phone, but had been trying to hack a GPS system to track the second Lexus.

"Got it," Robin said after a moment. "Coming at your position in thirty seconds."

"Thanks," Pickett said. "Stick with us, we're going to hang back some and try to not spook the driver."

At that moment a white Lexus SUV went past in front of them.

Ben was driving.

Pickett took her time pulling into traffic behind him. Since Robin had him tracking on GPS, they could take a few more chances. And that was a relief.

"Cavanaugh," Sarge said into the radio.

"Go ahead," Cavanaugh said.

"We have picked up Ben driving the second car, heading into town."

"Good work," Cavanaugh said. "Stay on him. Let us know if he is coming this way."

"Understood," Sarge said.

"I'm betting he's not," Robin said. "I've been listening to the conversation and Cathy was bragging about how she had put on a show for Ben in front of the police."

"So where is Ben heading?" Pickett asked.

Sarge shook his head. "He was a man totally in love with Cathy and willing to overlook a lot."

Pickett nodded to that. She had sensed the same thing about Ben, which was why she was hoping Cathy and Ben weren't involved.

"My sense," Sarge said, "is that our visit forced him to put two and two together and finally decide he can't deal with anymore. He's not going to join them. Maybe he's headed for the airport to leave her."

Pickett nodded. That made perfect sense.

"Or he's going to jump onto the freeway and just head to California," Sarge said.

Pickett nodded to that as well. "If he starts to do that, we're going to need the state police to stop and arrest him before he gets to the border."

"Let's see where he's headed first," Sarge said. "There might be something else going on here."

Pickett nodded.

Sarge laughed. "With this case, I think that's the norm, not the unusual."

Pickett agreed with that completely. So far they had been totally wrong about Cathy. There was a very good chance they were wrong about Ben on this as well.

They were soon going to know. More than likely in two more stoplights.

"How is the meeting going?" Sarge asked Robin.

"Kevin is telling his part of the story about his meetings with you two and then the three of you," Robin said.

At that point, Ben in the Lexus in front of them hit the stoplight. A right turn would take him to the airport or the freeway out of town. A left turn would take him in the direction of the house.

He went straight instead.

"Not a clue what he is doing," Sarge said.

They followed him for another ten minutes until finally the white Lexus pulled into the parking lot of Love Lost Mortuary and Crematorium.

"Damn it all to hell," Sarge said.

"I am pulling up security cameras on the place," Robin said. "I'll forward them to your phone, Pickett. Sarge, you keep your phone open on speaker."

"Understood," Sarge said.

He really liked how the three of them worked as a team and tonight the teamwork was proving invaluable.

Pickett got parked just a half block down the street from the mortuary and the car shut down. At that moment her phone beeped and she clicked it on.

She showed Sarge the images that Robin was forwarding.

Ben had climbed out of his car and had gone to the back door and was unlocking it.

"Do they own this thing?" Sarge asked.

"Got two of Will's people digging right now," Robin said.

Pickett watched as Ben went inside and the image on her phone switched to a camera inside to follow him.

"Cavanaugh?" Sarge said into the police radio.

"Go ahead," Cavanaugh said.

"Ben has stopped at a mortuary and crematorium and has entered it."

"What?" Cavanaugh said.

Pickett smiled as Sarge gave him the address. Then Sarge said, "We need an instant warrant for Robin to tap the security feed."

"Understood," Cavanaugh said. "You need backup?"

"Not yet," Sarge said. "We are just standing off and observing."

Cavanaugh signed off with a promise he would have the warrant at light speed.

Pickett just shook her head as Robin said, "Thank you."

"Stupid active cases have so many rules," Sarge said, grinning at Pickett.

Then they watched as Ben went into the crematorium part of the building and went through a procedure to heat up the ovens.

"Shit, he's going to cremate a body," Pickett said after watching for a moment.

"But what body?" Sarge asked.

Pickett had no response to that one. She had no idea.

CHAPTER THIRTY-TWO

June 16th, 2017
Las Vegas, Nevada

Sarge knew it took time to heat up the ovens to a temperature that would cremate a human body. And then the procedure took some time as well.

Ben went over to a chair against one wall, sat down, and picked up a magazine that was there on an end table and started to read.

Sarge was amazed that the guy seemed like he was in no hurry at all. He and his wife had no idea that they were surrounded by police.

And clearly Ben had done this before. He seemed comfortable with the procedure.

But Sarge still couldn't begin to figure out who Ben planned to cremate.

The warrant came through after only five minutes. Cavanaugh was right, it was light speed.

"I have trimmed off all the images I got from before the exact moment of the warrant," Robin said.

"Good work, partner," Pickett said. "What's happening at the house?"

"They are still talking money and business and websites and you name it," Robin said. "Going to be ugly for them in court because they actually talked about the damage one client had done to one of the bodies he dug up and how that had to be 'repaired' for the next client."

"Besides disgusting, how bad can we get all the clients on this?"

"Class D felonies," Robin said.

Sarge nodded. "Abuse of a corpse is usually a misdemeanor, but when sex is involved it becomes a felony. A sexual crime that can't be dropped from a record and is up to four years in jail per infraction."

Pickett looked at him with a puzzled look.

"Had a really nasty case about three years before I retired," Sarge said, smiling. "A guy killed his wife because she wouldn't have sex with him, then he kept her body around for a week, forcing himself on the body."

"Oh, yuck," Pickett said.

"The crap we have all seen," Robin said.

"This case ranks right up there on the crap meter," Sarge said.

Pickett could only agree with that.

"Looks like we might just be heading into new lands of crap on Cavanaugh's end," Robin said. "Cathy just asked her father and brother if they wanted to go have a little fun."

"How far will Cavanaugh let that go?" Pickett asked.

Sarge really didn't want to think about it and was very glad they weren't watching.

"As far as it takes to make sure no jury seeing the film would ever let them go," Robin said.

At that moment Ben glanced at his watch and stood and headed for the door.

Robin jumped the security cams to follow him until Ben got a rolling table to put a body on. Then he went back out to his car and opened the back.

"Holy shit, he has a body in there," Pickett said.

"Cavanaugh," Sarge said into the radio. "Send backup quietly. Ben has a body and is loading it onto a cart to cremate. We're going to need to stop him."

"Be damned careful," Cavanaugh said.

Sarge checked his gun and Pickett did the same.

They both stripped off their jackets so their badges were in plain sight.

Then they studied the image on Pickett's phone. Ben had managed to get a body out of the back of the SUV and loaded on the cart. It looked like a small woman's body.

He got the back door of the mortuary open again and went in, pushing the cart. He didn't seem to be concerned about being caught, from what Sarge could tell. This guy clearly must have done this a bunch of times, that was for sure.

"We don't dare wait for backup," Pickett said.

"Let's go," Sarge said, nodding.

"Cavanaugh," Sarge said into the radio, "tell the backup arriving that there are two detectives on the scene and in the building."

"Copy," Cavanaugh said.

Sarge put the radio on the seat.

Pickett nodded and they both climbed out, closing their doors slowly and quietly. The evening air was still warm from the day and the sounds of the neighborhood were only a dog barking and a car without a muffler in the distance.

This was not something he had expected to be doing tonight.

Or actually any night ever again.

But they simply had no choice.

CHAPTER THIRTY-THREE

June 16ᵗʰ, 2017
Las Vegas, Nevada

Pickett could feel the adrenaline rushing through her system as
they quickly ran around to the back of the building. She had her
phone with the security images still streaming to it and Robin
was on Sarge's phone. But at the moment both phones were in
their pockets and their guns were in their hands.

The back door had closed behind Ben and Sarge carefully
tested it.

"Locked," he whispered.

He took out his phone. "Robin, are the locks part of the
security system?"

Sarge said, "Thanks," and put the phone back in his pocket.

"Nope," he said to Pickett.

They both still carried their lock pick kits with them and
Sarge bent down quickly by the door while Pickett watched the
security feed.

"Ben's reached the cremation room," Pickett said, watching the video feed on her phone. If he went right to the oven with the body, they were going to need to hurry otherwise the body was going to be damaged and hard to identify.

Sarge quickly worked at the lock. Of the two of them, he was the fastest at picking locks and from the looks of it, the security lock on the mortuary would take him about a minute at best.

As she watched the security feed of Ben, he uncovered the body and took it out of the body bag.

It was a woman, looked to be around thirty, who had been embalmed and clearly been dead for a while and left in a dry, open place. Maybe over a year from the looks of the stage of mummification. Pickett didn't want to think about where this woman had been kept.

Or for what reason.

But as she watched, she realized she was going to get to see real quickly what the woman was being used for since Ben was also undressing.

"Oh, please hurry," Pickett said to Sarge.

"Why?" Sarge asked, not stopping his work on the door lock.

"Because Ben is about to have sex with the dead woman before he cremates her."

That stopped Sarge and he looked up at Pickett. "You are kidding me?"

"I am not," Pickett said.

She watched the image as Ben took off his clothes and moved toward the corpse.

"Any sign of a gun?" Sarge asked, working on the door.

"He's naked and about ten feet from his clothes," Pickett said. "The only thing he's armed with is disgusting."

Sarge laughed as he clicked open the door and stood.

At that moment two officers came around the building.

"Detectives Pickett and Carson," Pickett said to the cops in a loud whisper, showing them her badge. One cop was a man, the other a woman, and both looked young. In the faint light of the parking lot Pickett couldn't see their names.

"Follow us in," Sarge said. "We got a suspect in the crematorium with a body."

Both cops nodded.

"We don't think he is armed, but we take no chances," Sarge said.

Both nodded again.

Sarge went through the door first and went to the right while Pickett followed and went left.

The two cops followed, moving quietly as well, one stopping for a second to brace open the door.

Sarge took out his phone. "Robin, anything we should be worried about?"

"You are clear all the way to the event," Robin said. "Turn right into the hallway ahead and go about fifty paces to the door on the left."

He put the phone back in his pocket. "Robin says we are clear."

Pickett nodded, staring at the image over her phone. "Things are getting heated in the crematorium."

Sarge laughed and headed off, gun drawn, but down.

Pickett smiled at the two cops, then followed Sarge, her gun in one hand, the phone in the other. The two new cops were in for a story tonight that she was fairly certain they would never tell their children.

They made quick time in formation, as they had all been trained, down the hallway.

They spread out on both sides of the door to the crematorium.

Then Sarge carefully tried the door and discovered it was unlocked.

He held up one finger, then two, then three, and he went in first.

Pickett had the phone put away in her pocket and she went in beside Sarge.

The two cops came in behind them and went either direction along the wall.

The room smelled hot from the oven fire and had a slight gas tint to the air.

The gurney with the body was smack in the middle of the room, the woman's corpse facing upward.

Ben was facing downward.

Ben looked up from where he was, lying on top of the mummified woman's body. He seemed stunned and a little confused.

"Please get down with your hands in the air," Sarge said, moving to Ben's right.

Pickett, with her gun trained on Ben, went to the left.

The two patrol officers stayed put against the wall near the door.

Ben did as asked, clearly aroused from what he had been doing.

"Lie face down on the floor and put your hands behind your head.

Ben went slowly to his knees, then down to the floor and put his hands behind his head.

"Officer, cuff him please," Sarge said.

The woman officer nodded and came up and put a knee in

the middle of Ben's back, pressing him and his erection down against the hard floor, then roughly cuffed him.

"Make sure he doesn't make a move," Pickett said to the young woman officer.

The young officer glanced at the mummified body of the woman on the table, then at Ben on the floor, and said, "He makes a move and I'll step on his dick with my boots."

Pickett and Sarge both laughed as Ben jerked.

Sarge took out his phone and said, "Tell Cavanaugh we are clear here and Ben is in custody."

Sarge nodded, laughed, and put the phone back in his pocket.

"Officer," Sarge said to the guy still beside the door, clearly looking like he was in shock, "please go back to the parking lot and escort the detectives that are arriving in here."

The officer nodded and left, looking very relieved.

"Cavanaugh already knows," Sarge said to Pickett. "And Robin is going to stream the show going on at the other house to your phone. She said it's about to get interesting and they are getting ready to go in."

Pickett pulled out her phone as the image switched.

Kevin and an older man were getting undressed in a bedroom that looked like a master bedroom beside a huge king bed. A corpse of a woman with brunette hair was in the bed, under the covers.

The old guy looked to be almost eighty and starting to get frail.

As the two men finished getting undressed and were standing beside the bed, Cathy came into the room, also naked.

But there was one thing she had with her that no one expected. A very nasty looking pistol with what looked to be a sound suppressor on it.

Robin had streamed the audio as well, so when Cathy came into the room, Pickett heard her say, "Let's really have some fun, shall we?"

Both men nodded.

"Pull back the covers and climb in there with that young woman," Cathy said to the two men.

They did. Her brother had an erection. Her father did not.

The woman was completely mummified and her legs were spread.

"Great," Cathy said. Then she shot her brother once in the head, then her father before he could even move.

Both Pickett and Sarge jumped at that.

Pickett had not seen that coming.

"Holy shit," Sarge said.

"Damn that was fun," Cathy said. "Now I can have some real fun."

She put the gun on the dresser near the door and climbed into the bed with the three bodies. And before Cavanaugh and his men could get there, she was completely covered in blood.

CHAPTER THIRTY-FOUR

June 30th, 2017
Las Vegas, Nevada

For the first four days after all the arrests, the press had kept everything quiet about finding bodies in all the houses. Sarge had been impressed they had held off that long.

As many families as possible had been notified before the press had started to talk about the mess, but even after the first little bit, the press was focusing on helping find families instead of the sensationalism of the entire crimes.

In fact, most of the facts about the sexual ring were kept tight and around the country arrest warrants were being issued for the clients that had used those houses over the last fifteen years.

Ben and Cathy had really helped with that, since all the clients had been recorded and files had been carefully kept by Ben, including photographs.

And, as Cavanaugh had suggested, many of the men

arrested had been put into general population of a prison to be held for extradition. It seemed that having sex with the dead bodies of women tended to upset even the most hardened criminals and police officers.

Turned out that many of the clients were not in good enough health after a short time in jail to be extradited. Both Sarge and Pickett found that wonderfully funny.

On the day after the raids, with a search warrant on Ben and Cathy's home, Cavanaugh and the other detectives had also found two more women's bodies in a hidden room in the basement. One was a missing person's woman from about a year ago, the most recent of all the murders.

Sarge was very glad that he and Pickett were off the case after arresting Ben. They had just spent the time relaxing, watching movies, exercising some, and eating far too much.

Ben and Cathy had their pictures splashed all over the newspapers around the country as the "Necrophilia Killers." And Ben's books and art suddenly vanished from art galleries and stores.

He had become famous, but not for his art.

Now, finally, after a pretty good countdown, it was Cavanaugh's last day as an active detective and tomorrow would be his first as an active member of the Cold Poker Gang Task Force.

So Pickett and Sarge were throwing him a party at their place with all the gang coming, and he was also getting a party at the station before he left there.

Cavanaugh had called it a "goodbye–hello" kind of day.

Sarge and Pickett, with the help of Robin and Will, had brought in food and a massive cake. And had even locked the cats in a back bedroom in Pickett's side of the condo just so they wouldn't accidently escape.

Even the Chief of Police was stopping by to officially make Cavanaugh a member of the Gang.

Outside, the evening was warm, but not bad for the middle of the summer. In a few hours they all might be able to actually sit on the balcony upstairs. That balcony had almost a three-hundred-degree view of the entire valley, including right down the Strip. Best view in all of the city as far as Sarge was concerned. The main reason he had bought the condo in the first place.

Robin and Will were upstairs, setting up the cake and the table, and Sarge and Pickett were in the kitchen working on putting out the last of the food trays they had bought.

The condo smelled of fresh bread and deli meats.

Sarge felt they were about ready and it was still a half hour before people would start arriving.

"You know," Pickett said as she finished the last tray of meats, "I can't believe how lucky we are."

"Lucky how?" Sarge said. "You mean how lucky we are to be rich and in this place."

Pickett laughed and said, "Yeah, that too, but lucky to have each other and all these friends we work with."

"I agree," Sarge said, going over to her and hugging her. "What brought that up?"

"All this," Pickett said, "the party, everything. But I was just thinking how lucky I was to still be working as a detective. And working beside the man I love as a partner."

Sarge kissed her again. "I feel the same way."

At that moment there was a knock at the door and Cavanaugh entered. He saw them standing, holding each other in the kitchen, and shook his head.

"Haven't we had enough dead-people sex for one month?"

"Oh, trust me, Cavanaugh," Pickett said, "our sex is far, far from dead."

"What did I just hear?" Robin asked as she came down the stairs toward the kitchen.

"Far, far too much information for my young ears," Cavanaugh said, laughing as Robin went to him for a hug.

Pickett hugged him as well and then Sarge shook his hand. "Congratulations, you made it to the light side."

"The no-paperwork zone," Cavanaugh said, laughing. "It took me most of yesterday just to tell the two young detectives who are taking over that last case what paperwork hadn't been done yet."

"Oh, that's just evil," Pickett said, laughing.

"They'll just do it to other young detectives when they retire," Cavanaugh said.

Sarge just laughed and remembered that he had done the same thing the last day before he had retired as well.

Over the next thirty minutes most of the other fifteen Cold Poker Gang members arrived, some with spouses. And the chief arrived and congratulated Cavanaugh on the transition.

"Welcome aboard the task force," Sarge said to Cavanaugh. "I hope you can play poker and like to lose money."

"I play poker just fine," Cavanaugh said. "But not to lose money. And you guys actually play poker?"

"We do," Pickett said. "Some better than others."

"Just bring enough cash each week," Sarge said, smiling at Cavanaugh. "And you'll fit in just fine."

"And to think I thought this task force would be all fun and games," Cavanaugh said, smiling.

At that everyone laughed and the Cold Poker Gang gained one great new member.

And the food and the drinks and the laughing lasted well into the night. Not bad for a bunch of old retired people.

The Cold Poker Gang Mysteries continue with the next book in the series, Heads Up. *Following is a sample chapter from that book.*

January 17th, 2019
Las Vegas, Nevada

The old Hotel Nevada on Main Street in downtown Las Vegas seemed to be in hiding, almost ashamed to be seen. Only its seven-story oblong tower and a walled-off portion of the old casino was left standing. All the big Nevada-shaped signs with big "N" logos that used to cover the Main Street corner were gone, as well as the huge neon "Nevada" sign that had run across the top of the building proudly telling the world the Hotel Nevada existed.

Every entry on the ground floor had been walled in like a bad horror movie and painted a neutral light-gold color to match exactly the paint color of the entire building. Those old entrances looked as if they had always been walls.

Large, bright-colored billboards along street level now advertised restaurants, steaks, drinks, and gambling at the nearby Golden Nugget, the current owner of the old hotel. Those signs seemed to mock the remains of Hotel Nevada like memories of its past.

The ground floor casino area that used to front Main Street was now mostly a Golden Gate Casino parking lot, not even a bump in the pavement left of where millions were won and lost.

Driving past on Main Street, unless you knew the empty building used to be a major downtown Las Vegas casino, you would never notice it.

No one ever did.

It sat lost.

Hidden in plain sight.

All the room windows from the second floor up still had their drapes and looked like people might actually be in those rooms or sitting on the balconies of the seven-floor building.

No one ever was.

Some days a few of the windows were opened to air the floors out, causing the curtains to blow like ghosts. But there was no way at all into the building besides a heavy steel security door hidden in an alley near a large parking garage.

The Hotel Nevada sat empty.

Alone.

And completely ignored by everyone.

Recently retired Detective Benson Cavanaugh had gone past the old hotel a hundred times since it had been shuttered in 2012 and never gave the place a second thought.

At least not until tonight.

Now he held a red cold-case file with a picture of the old hotel before it was shuttered and what the hotel had looked like a few years ago, which is what it looked like still today. Why someone had thought to take a picture of the ghost hotel was beyond him.

Around Cavanaugh in the basement game room, fifteen or more retired detectives were talking, laughing, or staring at their cards. Two large poker tables filled the game room of retired detectives Bayard Lott and Julia Rogers. A polished wooden bar from an old hotel filled one wall, and recessed lighting over the bar and the poker tables kept the room bright and yet homey-looking.

The room was climate controlled and even with that many old people in it, the air didn't feel stuffy or warm. And no one smoked, so the air was breathable.

Cavanaugh had fallen in love with the room the moment he had come down the stairs. One of those rooms you wish you had in your own home, but never could afford or find the time to put in.

Bowls of chips and M&Ms were scattered around the room and most everyone had a drink of some sort in front of them, a lot of it soda or water. These were all old detectives. Drinking alcohol, other than a beer or two, for most of them was a thing long in their past.

Cavanaugh felt the same way. He couldn't remember the last time he had had a drink past a small glass of wine at a good dinner.

Hell, he couldn't remember the last time he had gone out for a good dinner, actually.

The entire house had a faint smell of KFC. Cavanaugh had heard that Lott and Julia were KFC fans, but hadn't believed it until coming through the front door. That smell was easy to identify and damned hard to ignore.

Now he wished he would have eaten before coming. Chips just weren't going to hold him for long.

Cavanaugh could tell where there used to be a large-screen television on one wall, but Lott had told him it had been removed along with a couch and chair to make room for the second poker table as the Cold Poker Gang Task Force got bigger and more retired detectives wanted to actually play some poker each week.

Cavanaugh was the newest member of the task force. In fact, tonight was his first time at this regular Tuesday night meeting after just retiring from active duty and the tons of paperwork that went along with being a modern detective.

He had hated the paperwork. He knew of no detective who loved it, actually. But he flat loved the idea that on this special task force all they did was investigate and leave the paperwork to the active detectives when something was found.

Detective heaven as far as Cavanaugh was concerned.

Now, looking around at the room of retired detectives, he understood why they called this task force the Cold Poker Gang. Many of them actually played poker once a week and talked about the cold cases they were working on.

And Cavanaugh knew from his recent days as an active detective that this group closed a lot of cold cases and was respected throughout the city. And the Chief of Police backed the group completely while at the same time making sure it stayed out of the limelight.

Lott, the owner of this house, was sitting at one table, looking very serious at the play going on in front of him. Julia, his wife and partner, stood on the other side of the second table laughing with two other detectives. Lott and Julia had become a couple while starting this cold case task force. They and Retired Detective Andor Williams now ran it.

Andor actually did all the work connecting the task force with the Chief of Police and getting the cold cases to hand out. If there was a problem or question, Cavanaugh was supposed to immediately contact Andor.

Cavanaugh had been standing at the bar for a good thirty minutes, just trying to soak in everything after the wonderful welcome he had gotten when he arrived. He felt like he belonged here.

Then, out of the blue, Andor, a short square man with wide shoulders and a bald head, had handed an official-looking red case file to Cavanaugh.

Cavanaugh would have sworn it was an original case file if not for the large red word "copy" stenciled on the cover.

"Glance at this file and I'll be right back," Andor had said, then turned away.

Andor was the oldest of the active Cold Poker Gang at

seventy-three, but you could never tell he was that old. His energy was amazing and he walked anywhere like he would plow through a person in his way. Cavanaugh had heard of Andor and Lott solving some of the city's toughest cases back in the day when they were active partners.

Most of the detectives in the task force were in their late fifties and early sixties. Cavanaugh had retired at sixty-two with full benefits and health care, but he doubted he would have done that without knowing he could join this task force when he did.

Basically work was all he did in his life, all he had, and he loved it.

Cavanaugh knew most of the detectives in the room, if not personally, then by their fantastic reputations. Even though he felt welcome, he wasn't sure he belonged here with this caliber of detectives, but Lott and Julia and Andor had said he did, so Cavanaugh was going to give it a try.

Besides, he had nothing else to do. If he could solve cases working as a detective and not have to do the paperwork, he figured he didn't have much to lose.

But the case that Andor had handed him looked damn near impossible. A simple missing person's case of a Myra Stemple, age 23 when last seen coming out of a hotel on the Strip in 2009.

And even stranger was that her shoes, clothes, and purse, still holding over three hundred in cash, had been found three years later hidden in the back of a closet in the Hotel Nevada when it was being shuttered.

How the hell did that stuff get there? And how had it remained hidden for three years? Or had it just been put there a few days before? No way of knowing.

Or knowing what had happened to Myra.

That was clearly what Andor wanted Cavanaugh to find out.

Cavanaugh found it amazing those clothes and personal items had even been connected to a three-year-old missing person's case. Someone had been on the ball to manage that much.

Clearly the detectives on the case had done as much as they could, running into blank walls all the way along.

The case had been cold since 2012, but twice a year Myra Stemple's brother, a local attorney, went into the main station and talked to the detectives about the progress on his sister's case. More than likely his doing that got the case here to this task force.

At that moment Andor came back leading another detective who had been talking to Julia earlier. Cavanaugh recognized the new detective from seeing her regularly in the Main Street Station Casino buffet. He had had no idea until tonight she was a detective.

"Cavanaugh," Andor said, "meet Retired Detective Bonnie State."

"Great meeting you," Bonnie said, smiling.

Cavanaugh somehow managed to say, "Nice meeting you."

Up close, Bonnie was one of the most attractive women he had seen in a long time. She had short brown hair, rich brown eyes, and a long face that looked like it smiled a lot. She was fairly tall, maybe only a few inches shorter than his six-two and she looked trim, like she worked out a lot, maybe even as a runner.

She had on jeans, tennis shoes, and a white blouse under a light tan blazer. He had no idea how old she was since her face showed very few wrinkles, but she was clearly old enough to be a retired detective.

And there seemed to be a force of energy around her. He liked that.

He reached out his hand and she shook it, her grip firm. She looked directly at him at that moment, then said, "Have we met?"

He laughed as he let go of her hand, even though a part of him didn't want to. "Trust me, I would have remembered, even at this advanced age."

He didn't say anything about seeing her a number of times in the buffet.

She laughed as well and blushed slightly.

Her laugh was wonderful, with a slight force to it that he had a hunch went with her energy and was part of her personality.

"Since you two are the new kids on the block," Andor said.

"I love it when someone calls me a new kid," Cavanaugh said, interrupting Andor.

Bonnie laughed and said, "Yeah, me too. Makes me feel all young and tingly again."

Cavanaugh just nodded. "Ah, to be young and tingly. Those were the good old days."

"Sure do miss the young part," Bonnie said.

"The tingly part wasn't bad either."

Andor just went on ignoring them both, "You two are now partners."

That statement took all the fun out of the air like a bad fart in a crowded elevator.

"I work alone," Cavanaugh said, suddenly feeling a little panicked.

No, scratch that. A lot panicked.

"So have I," Bonnie said. "Last ten years."

"Not on this task force," Andor said, smiling at both of them. "We work in teams of two or three, three being better since no telling when one of us is going to fall and break a hip. So get used to it."

Andor tapped the case file Cavanaugh had been looking at. "Sorry about that one right off. Someone had to take it. You two were just unlucky enough on the draw is all."

With that Andor turned and walked away, leaving the two of them standing there side-by-side, their mouths open.

Cavanaugh couldn't believe it. Twelve years as a detective working alone and now that he was retired, he ended up with a partner.

This did not bode well at all.

NEWSLETTER SIGN-UP

Be the first to know!

Just sign up for the Dean Wesley Smith newsletter, and keep up with the latest news, releases and so much more—even the occasional giveaway.

So, what are you waiting for? To sign up go to deanwesleysmith.com.

But wait! There's more. Sign up for the WMG Publishing newsletter, too, and get the latest news and releases from all of the WMG authors and lines, including Kristine Kathryn Rusch, Kristine Grayson, Kris Nelscott, *Fiction River: An Original Anthology Magazine, Smith's Monthly*, and so much more.

To sign up go to wmgpublishing.com.

ABOUT THE AUTHOR

Considered one of the most prolific writers working in modern fiction, *USA Today* bestselling writer Dean Wesley Smith published far more than a hundred novels in forty years, and hundreds of short stories across many genres.

At the moment he produces novels in several major series, including the time travel Thunder Mountain novels set in the Old West, the galaxy-spanning Seeders Universe series, the urban fantasy Ghost of a Chance series, a superhero series starring Poker Boy, and a mystery series featuring the retired detectives of the Cold Poker Gang.

His monthly magazine, *Smith's Monthly*, which consists of only his own fiction, premiered in October 2013 and offers readers more than 70,000 words per issue, including a new and original novel every month.

During his career, Dean also wrote a couple dozen *Star Trek* novels, the only two original *Men in Black* novels, Spider-Man and X-Men novels, plus novels set in gaming and television worlds. Writing with his wife Kristine Kathryn Rusch under the name Kathryn Wesley, he wrote the novel for the NBC miniseries The Tenth Kingdom and other books for *Hallmark Hall of Fame* movies.

He wrote novels under dozens of pen names in the worlds of comic books and movies, including novelizations of almost a dozen films, from *The Final Fantasy* to *Steel* to *Rundown*.

Dean also worked as a fiction editor off and on, starting at Pulphouse Publishing, then at *VB Tech Journal*, then Pocket Books, and now at WMG Publishing, where he and Kristine Kathryn Rusch serve as series editors for the acclaimed *Fiction River* anthology series.

For more information about Dean's books and ongoing projects, please visit his website at www.deanwesleysmith.com and sign up for his newsletter.

For more information:
www.deanwesleysmith.com

www.ingramcontent.com/pod-product-compliance
Lightning Source LLC
Chambersburg PA
CBHW010736100726
47899CB00009B/3071